DE ANGELES & KNIGHT

THE SKELLIG

LY DE ANGELES

&
MELAINE KNIGHT

DE ANGELES & KNIGHT

THE SKELLIG

ISBN – 1974154483

Author—Ly de Angeles
Website—www.lydeangeles.com

Editor/Additional Vision/Graphics—Melaine Knight,
The Neon Rebel www.rebel-rebel.com.au

Cover—Melaine Knight and Liz Bonney

Thanks to Dr Iris Curteis for a terrific critical review

ALSO BY DE ANGELES —

The Way of the Goddess, Prism/Unity, 1987

The Way of Merlyn, Prism/Unity, 1990

Witchcraft Theory and Practice, Llewellyn Worldwide, 2000

The Feast of Flesh and Spirit, Wildwood Gate, 2001

When I See the Wild God, Llewellyn Worldwide, 2002

Pagan Visions, Llewellyn Worldwide, 2004

The Quickening, Llewellyn Worldwide, 2005

The Shining Isle, Llewellyn Worldwide, 2006

Tarot Theory and Practice, Llewellyn Worldwide, 2007

Magdalene, C2012

The Quickening, Revised, 2012

The Shining Isle, Revised, 2012

Comeuppance, The Crime Factory, 2014

Priteni, the Decimation of the Indigenous Celtic Britons, 2015

Initiation, a Memoir, 2016

Witch, 2017

Genesis, The Furure2018

Please note that any word the reader does not understand

can be found on the Internet.

THE SKELLIG

Prologue

The Year of 2156 According to the Gregorian Calendar

(Gamble)

SOME PEOPLE CALL ME *Little Earth*. It's an endearment, not my name. Most of the time I'm a gorgeous, thirty-something year old woman, and sometimes, at the turn of the moon, I'm a fucken enormous praying mantis. A shapeshifter, yes. Appearances, however, can be deceiving because I'm positively ancient.

Once I was a rocky outcrop on a tiny island in the sea off the coast of Ireland. Home to birds and moss and not much else. But I've been around people forever, it sometimes seems. Most of them, at the time of writing this account of history, are now nasty. And the saddest thing is that for countless centuries they were not.

I remember them the night before a big hunt. The old women dressed in antlers and skins still hung with polished hooves, singing the songs to summon the herd, dancing the dance of the species whose garments they wore. Invoking wind and weather and the voices of ravens, to tell of the run come daylight. Down below the snow line. Through eerie fog, and foot-deep snow that says nothing. Startling at the crack of high branches blowing in an invisible wind. An endless forest of ash and spruce and birch.

Descending the cliff face, following a waterfall frozen in time, to the valley and out onto the plains. And here they come! Vying with wolves, the hunters begin the long lope as the vast herd tears up ancient sod and strikes sparks off cleared granite where the sun has melted the thinner freeze to hoar slush. Spears are black lines against a white sky, taking down an adolescent buck. Him dropping dead from one shot, perfectly aimed, that pierces deeply to within muscle and organs just behind the foreleg. Into the heart. The hunters gut him, thanking him for being the one. Honoring him. The hot liver is bitten, first by the hunter that made the kill and then shared. The intestine is emptied, its innards left for crows and ants and whoever else lives close enough to smell the blood. The carcass is carried back to the village where everything is put to use and every person sings the event into memory; love songs sung to Mother Caribou and her multitude of children down the ages.

Now is compassionless and ignorant. The consensus du jour, that earth is deemed tamed. Depends on what side of the tracks a body is born onto though, doesn't it? An illusion, of course. The biggest deception of all, however, is that in the old days lions and tigers and wolves and bears were to be feared when all they did was hunt and kill their dinner. In that long ago before the second great extinction.

No more caribou now. The last of them died on the side of a highway what? A hundred years ago? Nor wolves, either. They got done with bullets. Or baits, along with every critter that scavenged the remains. No. Livestock are penned and fattened until slaughter. No more food free to roam. Only knowing mud and feces. They are not thought to possess emotion. To want to nurture their young. They are merely prepackaged meat. The species still technically resembling animals, that is. The problem is that science has learned to do what once only sorcery and magic could.

I get distracted, so shoot me. Sex is a wonderful thing, as is moonshine, as is the art of cussing in every known language. I have no regret at being what I am. No regret at all.

1

On Being a Skellig in a World Gone Bad

(Gamble)

SHUDDERING UNCONTROLLABLY. My eyes are wide open and there's nothing. Black. Trying to take in light that's non-existent. My breath hits the lid of the box and bounces back at me like an echo. Teeth clack maddeningly with every pot hole. My ankles are zip tied. My hands also, bound behind my back, alive with the venom of pins and needles and I push tentatively against all sides of this prison with my elbows. To no avail. Oak. I know oak when I smell it. No busting outa this.

How could I have fallen asleep there? A mortal's pub for goodness sake.

Here we go again, I think. *They won't know what I am, and they'll send me to another flipping laboratory. Tests and probes. And it'll take me another two days to shape-change fully back because the black moon's just yesterday and how's that for the luck of the Irish?*

'Ow!'

The box is dropped from a great height, and I smash into the lid on impact. Blood trickles into my ear from my nose. I tip my face sideways and it drains out and pools under my cheek. My hands burn with the pain.

Nails finally scream in submission to the crowbar that jimmies the lid. Floodlight ransacks the inside dark and I have to squint in self-defense. I feign dead, but I observe through sly eyelashes.

One big bloke looks like his nose has been busted about a thousand times and the other, tiny and greasy, has boils on his forehead and open pores like moon craters. I open my eyes fully and stare them down. The big bloke snorts derision at my bravado and grabs my hands. I wish I could spit but there's nothing wet about me.

'Get its feet.'

Boils does as he's told.

Don't think, don't over-think it, I think. *Keep calm. Wait. Wait.*

I struggle like crazy, but it just hurts more and forces me to drop my wings onto the tarmac through the effort. I play dead again but not before I reconnoiter the surroundings for an escape.

We're at a stainless-steel entrance, like a closed trap, to the biggest blandest research lab I've ever been dragged to. I'm dumped on the concrete step, my face sideways to Boil's boot. I twist my head up when Potato Nose rings the buzzer. We're under the surveillance orbs of several security cameras but we still seem to wait an age. Bounty hunters are not your pristine city blokes. Probably hard to identify beneath the grease.

Eventually a good looking young guy, maybe twenty-five, maybe thirty, with a haircut worth a second glance, opens the door to a huff of icy, antiseptic air.

'Can I help you?' Soft voice. Deep, with a bit of honey and gravel to it. I watch the boot through eye slits.

'The reward,' says Nose.

'It's a stick insect hybrid.' Good Hair squats and scrutinizes my bits; rubs a hand gently along my carapace.

'It's *someone's* hybrid. Don't care who takes it.'

'It's a she by the way,' He stands and shoves his hands in his pockets.

'You paying? Or shall my friend and I do business elsewhere?'

'It'll be up to my supervisor. Wait here.'

The door seals hermetically behind him. Boils toes me in the neck and I breathe a druid curse onto him. One wing is bent the wrong way and the pain's nasty.

'Arrogant little prick,' spits Nose pointlessly towards the closed door.

Then, again with inside air and two pair of feet and legs, sneakers and boots, but both in jeans and one in a lab coat, stand near my face.

'How do I know it's not a fallout mutation from the barrens?' The legs under the lab coat shuffle.

'Do we look idiots?' growls Nose. 'It was asleep at a pub in Dodge. It's playing dead. Force its eyes open. The eyes give it away.'

I turn my face up. It's the good hair guy.

'I'll pay you two quid,' says the other one, Labcoat.

'Bollocks,' says Nose. 'It's worth twenty and you know it.'

'*Sir*, old boy. You can call me *Sir*,' says Labcoat.

'It's worth twenty... *Sir*.'

Labcoat leans down sideways and studies my face. I will myself to look phasmid, insectoid, and invisible. I know he knows though.

'I'd speculate it's from the discarded batch back in the thirties.

They were all insect hybrids that decade. Cheap thrills for the customers. The praying mantis bobbing on the curtains was always good for a laugh.'

'She looks young,' says Good Hair.

Labcoat stands and fishes out his wallet, slipping a twenty-cred voucher to Nose.

A look passes between him and Boils that says he should have asked for more.

Yeah, go on, fuck off.

I lie there helpless while Good Hair and Labcoat take their goddamn time, with their hands in their pockets and their eyes all over me.

Labcoat takes hold of my feet, making sure to bend his knees when he lifts. Good Hair grabs me under the arms. Poor bastard's the one has to walk backwards along the corridor. He's got a bluebird tattoo on his left hand, on the meat between his thumb and forefinger. Thought that was illegal. Must be from old money to get away with that little rebellion.

Labcoat checks his handheld and strips off the whites, stuffing them into a big square stainless-steel trolley with a purple plastic hazmat bag suspended from it. 'I've got a jolly good fuck in half an hour. I'm going to leave you to run the checks. It'll have to get put down. If it escaped once, it'll do it again. They were all capable of learning.'

'Yes, sir.'

I know what he's talking about. I know all about it. All those genetic experiments. If only they hadn't made ones that look like me this wouldn't be happening. I would still be thought imaginary.

Fuck. Think!

I'm dragged through a plastic door and I panic. It's an autopsy room and I'm hauled onto the coldest slab of metal in the world. We're under stark neon and I'd kill for moonlight.

Labcoat outs the room and Good Hair clicks on the three hundred watt lamp at the end of its white plastic retractractable arm.

With an overly enormous and intimidating magnifying lens. That he hovers just above my face.

I look up at Good Hair's eye. It's as wide as a dinner plate, so I don't know what he can see. My brain maybe.

'Please let me go.'

He staggers backward. Falls against the bench and a tray load of instruments go flying. He stumbles and rights himself, disbelief written all over his face. It's funny, but I suppress the smile I know he would not appreciate. He doesn't realize his mouth is hanging off its hinge.

'Please?' I implore.

He inches towards me. 'You can talk.'

'What about begging is beyond you?' I ask. I want to tell myself to keep the sarcasm down, but this is so tedious.

I bat my eyelashes.

He blinks again. How long can silence take? It's a standoff and I can't afford to back down. He's a mortal and that's always a definite disadvantage when you're me.

'You're just supposed to chirrup,' he whispers.

I swing my legs over the edge of the slab and the relief is instantaneous. My wings. The pressure of even my own body for that long.

'So, can I go?'

He leans over until I can smell him. He's had garlic for lunch but

I'm not about to comment.

He looks me in the eye. 'No.'

By now I'm getting really itchy. It's at least a day since I wore skin and being trapped away from the elements dries me out.

'Well can I have a shower?'

'I. Um. What?'

'I'm trying really hard to be nice when it really isn't in my nature. Do you realize that?'

He does this kind of leaning thing in an attempt to look cool. Cute. I grin. No idea what that looks like from his perspective.

'Can I?'

Eyes. Him at mine. Mine at his. His are the color of storms.

'Shower,' I whisper, 'I'm in a bad way here.'

He continues scrutinizing me and says nothing. It's like he's a bit dull which is unfortunate for a scientist. I wonder if there are monkeys here, tied to chairs with their skulls removable like in another lab I escaped from once. Research wires, computers and cages. Lights this bright. Permanent deserts but with aircon.

'Okay. But you're weirding me out you know.'

'I don't care. I itch.'

He gets me to my feet like he expects trouble but I'm all pliant and helpful and ready to bolt as soon as he gets that fucking door open.

Then the bastard only cuts the zip ties at my ankles. I'm sure my hands are about to fall off.

Then he leashes me! Collar and all. He attaches the strap on the other end to his wrist so that if I run, I'll be dragging a six-foot-something cute lab guy with good hair with me. I weigh up the situation. Could be worse.

H bicornis Hymenopus coronatus
Phasmid, Walking Flower Mantis, Orchid Mantis

2

Deliverance

(Gamble)

THE SHOWER IS HOT. THE STEAM exquisite; my wings relaxing under the mist. Good Hair, ever the scientist, observes me clinically from his end of my bondage. His eyes widen, however, when the water transforms my paper-seeming wings to iridescence. Colors that change from dung brown to autumn around an azure lake. I also feel more skin than shell and that's just a tad embarrassing. Unsure of what he sees. I avert my eyes and step out of the cubicle.

'Do I dry you?'

'I need to stay a little bit wet. What now?'

He shuffles.

'You don't have to do it. You could just let me go. I swear to all that's important I won't get pissed again let alone get caught. I swear on my grandmother's grave I won't say a word to anyone about you. Your boss won't know. How would he know? I'm a Rosy Maple moth what got no mouth. Shtum as they come. Seriously capable of keeping this entire episode to myself. Please? Please, please, please?'

'Dear god, can you just shut up?'

'I'm sentient.'

'And I'm not stupid.'

'I'm a skellig.

'What?'

'I'll explain if you let me go.'

He runs his fingers through his hair and rubs his baby-faced beard fuzz.

'Come with me,' I cajole. 'I can show you wonder.'

'My life's on the line here. And what makes you think I don't know about wonder.'

'You know you can't kill me.'

In this place of chrome and white and plastic and fake air he decides.

'And the correct term is euthanize. We don't use kill. But no, I can't.'

I continue eye contact knowing that what he said could mean anything.

He sits on the sterile tiled floor and just thinks. I shuffle. I put a hand on a hip. I drop my arms to my side. I fluff my wings a little. I work a crick out of my carapace. Feel the change beginning.

I can't stand it anymore. 'What?!'

'Give me a moment to work on a plan, for goodness sake.'

He scrutinizes the floor. Gazes blankly back at me. Sighs.

'What do I call you?'

'Gamble.'

'On what?'

'It's my name, not a vice. What's yours?'

'Terrence.'

'Terrence!' I smile. 'You look like a Terrence.' All charm.

He chews the inside of his cheek. 'I have a mind, Gamble. And when left in peace and quiet it is capable of mentally mapping an entire city. A thing I must do if we're to get you out of here. So please don't talk. If that's at all possible for you.'

I stare at the wall and imagine it's a window and I can see a vast horizon and mountains and freedom.

It seems like hours. I'm drying out again.

'What's in there,' I say eventually, indicating his head. I'm not good at discipline but I suppose that's, by now, obvious.

He slumps. Seems to shrink.

'What?'

'Well I've worked out a plan but not the consequences. And I must be nuts to even consider this.'

'What've you got to lose?'

'You're incorrigible. You don't know me. I have a life, little bug, and I'm actually considering stuffing with it because you fucking-well talk. I could get a promotion for finding this out.'

'I wouldn't say anything.'

'I've met you mere moments ago, oh strangely impossible creature, and I already ken that'd be impossible.'

'Wanna risk it?'

He stares at a corner of the ceiling as though it holds the answer. He checks his watch. He stands and undoes the leash and I turn my back to display the zip ties, my hands turning blue and white from lack of blood flow.

'I can feel gangrene setting in.'

'No, you can't. You're just lucky we're in the dead zone.'

'I have no idea…'

'If it wasn't three in the morning this entire complex would be bristling. The security shift's about to change and we have to go. Now.'

An elevator redeye sensor reads the inside of Terrence's wrist where the identity lozenge looks almost like a body-mod. We ride down in the elevator at a nauseating speed and it opens onto a stark deserted corridor.

We run. I'm scared. I'm light enough to make no noise whatsoever but I nearly lose the plot and laugh out loud because

Terrence's sneakers go squoick, squoick, squoick with every tip-toed step.

At the end of the corridor is another lift. Again, it's lozenge-only accessible. He swipes. We wait. It opens. We get in.

We drop so fast my ears pop before the elevator stops with a hush on a pocket of air and opens onto dark grey and concrete.

'We can't go out the main way,' he answers my unspokenness. I realize my face is in imploring mode.

We are in a vast concrete and steel storage facility that houses a gazillion cages, every conceivable dead piece of equipment and cast-off anything that looks like junk. Goes back centuries.

An enormous metal furnace glows fierce with white flame. I've never seen anything like it but my imagination makes the little prickles on my legs and arms stand up all creeped out.

'Don't ask,' he pleads.

Slaughter. Incineration. Get me outa here, Terrence.

He pulls me towards the sloping up-ramp and we run, keeping to the shadows, him looking out for security cameras the closer we get to what I assume will be a surface of the earth.

Clatter, crash, thump and the mumble of men's voices, the beep-beep of vehicles in reverse, the squawk, screech and scream of many a terrified animal.

I stare at Terrence in fear.

A sign announcing ARRIVAL AND DISPOSAL. 'What are you *doing?*' I hiss quietly.

Boxes, and shipping crates, and the dull, gun-metal grey of predawn beyond inside.

'Trust me,' he says.

Then black with texture.

I don't dare make a noise as I'm hoisted into a fireman's hold over my possible-traitor, possible-hero's shoulder.

'F23 from twelve,' Terrence yells at somebody.

'Down the chute,' the Somebody yells back.

'Nah, it's going to recycling.'

'Yeah, orrite. Outside, left, Dock Five. Too early for the truck though.'

First Terrence walks like he's got nothing better to do. I want to scream. Or bite his arm. Mostly, I want to be put down and have my hands untied. And run.

If wishes were horses…

Then he flips me and I'm in his arms and he's running and running.

Twists and turns of a maze and all the while, I'm as frightened and annoyed as any loser.

Trying to see out of the bag is not futile but it is intense. Little patches of the world in thread-size bites of grey.

Finally we stop, and he puts me on the ground and pulls the bag off my head and I'm getting pretty tired of having to adjust my eyesight so many times… And where are we exactly?

Outside yet another door. This one in a detritus-strewn alley out back of what smells like fake food and cheap cooking oil. Only enough room for bins and rats. And, it turns out, us. While he fumbles with the positively archaic, real keys I annoy myself by rationalizing that inside one of the buildings opposite is a trolley that will wheel those bins to a main drag somewhere (although the roar of engines, blare of horns, bone rattling rumble of drone swarms and the predictable screaming of cop cars and emergency vehicles inform me, it isn't that far away) because they look way too heavy for even a couple of big blokes. Nonsensically, they don't have handles.

Terrence eventually gets the heavy metal grid door unlocked and then the main door to what appears a very secure but dilapidated building.

He helps me to my feet before hurrying us into the linoleum-floored entrance to what turns out to be a boarded-up old theatre. He relocks everything behind us then leads the way backstage. There's more and more person happening in my body now. Twelve hours maybe? This could get awkward.

Behind the fraying scarlet curtains, amidst ropes that dangle from shot-out overhead floodlights suspended from a mass of girders, is his kitchen and his sofa and a sound system that's state-of-the-art and a big-screen plasma TV. Two guitars are on stands and there are stacks and stacks of books and comic books. He's even attached a basket up one of the poles for shooting hoops. On stage.

Now I haven't been surprised in a long, long time but this is unexpected.

He cuts the zip lock ties.

'Ow!'

'Paresthesia?'

'*What?*'

'Sorry, pins and needles?'

I'm too busily agonizing to answer the stupid question.

'You want a cup of coffee?'

I'm still too busy suffering. He waits patiently. What's that smile, Terrence? He thinks this is funny.

It takes another thirty seconds for the blood to settle but I keep the question at the forefront of the *what's-most-important-right-now* part of my brain.

'Is it real coffee?'

'Yes.'

'*Real* coffee?'

'Yes.'

'Yes. Please!'

Who is this guy that he can afford real coffee?

But he just stands there, his entire face changing to one of worry. Then he drops to his knees, runs his hands through that well-styled hair and grinds his teeth in kind of an ugly way. His eyes bug up a little and his eyebrows arch menacingly, almost painfully, towards that thin horizontal line on his forehead. And he holds his breath. It takes all of my willpower not to laugh, because I know it would be really inappropriate, but the full realization of what he has done is written all over him. The man don't need a mouth.

I perch on an upturned milk crate and wait for him to get over it, but he carries on for ages and in the end, I can't stand it anymore and I snort.

Then he lets his breath out in one quick rush and sucks in air like he's just surfaced from fathoms deep.

'And och! For a hybrid.'

'Am not.'

'If you're not then what on earth are you?'

'I've told you.'

'I know what you said. It's because you talk. And talk. And talk, that I'm in this abhorrent bleeding mess.'

'Once you've calmed down, and I've had that promised coffee, we can go get help.'

'Who from?'

'The others.'

'There are others?'

'Friends of mine with a bit more sophistication than I managed yesterday, surprise, surprise.'

'Others like you?'

'Depends what you mean by like. Why do you live in an abandoned theatre?'

'I inherited it.'

'It's a bit crappy.'

He doesn't say anything, so I shut up and let him work. He's like a maestro at the back wall where there are shelves and a sink and all the hoodoo of coffee making. He even grinds the beans.

'If this place is dero how come you've got electricity?'

'It's not, technically, electricity.'

'I won't ask.'

'It's interesting technology.'

'Does it take long to explain?'

'Probably.'

'Then no.'

The gas burner's on. The percolator is on. The cups and a spoon and a jar of sugar and a carton of milk and an open packet of Tim Tams are on the table.

3

Understanding

(Still Gamble)

I'M DEEP IN THOUGHT WHEN I'M handed a mug of coffee. 'So, what's this plan then, insect?'

'Now, no –'

'Sorry.'

I fluff my wings and blow on the java. I sip it cautiously in case it's crap but hey! Good hair and good coffee. I'm a little bit in love.

'We head for the badlands come nightfall,' I say.

'Dear god–

'C'mon! Hey, you're my hero. You'll see. It'll be worth your while. New things are interesting.'

'A skellig?'

'Sort of shape-shifter for the pleasure, curiosity or necessity. Immortalish. Originally part of a ragged bunch of rocks just off the coast of County Kerry in Ireland. Long time ago. Magical being.

Considered myth.'

'You don't sound Irish.'

'Neither do you.'

'I'm not. Stop it. This is just weird. Go again.'

'Good coffee by the way. Point score keeps going up, Terrence.'

'Please don't change the subject.'

'What's "the batch back in the thirties"?'

'It was tragic, Gamble. And, by the way, your human face looks maybe thirty, thirty-five. Quite pretty really.'

I think I'm blushing.

'Um. Where was I?' he continues, pink all down his neck like a stain of embarrassment. 'Yes. A genetic disaster. The experiments delved into the efficacy of HERVs.'

He watches what I presume is my empty, vacuous face.

'Human endogenous retroviruses. The experiments produced what's called a lentivirus that hadn't seen the light of day since... oh, I don't know, some Paleolithic ancestor fell into a crevasse in Norway or froze to death on the Altai Mountains. Or some modern silly wankery cross-breeding simians with human mammals. They were potentially as contagious as all get out—to people—and were quarantined. They'll likely all be euthanized at some stage, but government red tape takes years. You looked uncannily like one of them when you came in and it would have been a national emergency if you had been one.'

'Potentially? You mean an entire species was imprisoned for life, with the possibility of extermination?'

Terrence shrugs but avoids eye contact. He blows on his coffee and makes small slurpy sounds as he sips.

Then he places his cup on the floor and stands. Does this desperate foot-to-foot, jiggy-type move.

'You need to pee?' I say, hopefully. I still can't work out if he's peculiar.

'God, I am in so much trouble! When my supervisor finds out I'll be one fucking dead savant scientist. And he *will* find out, you know.'

'How much time do we have?'

'Only till morning.'

'When's that?'

Terrence checks the time. 'Now.'

'What do we do?'

'We leave.'

'How?'

He smiles with mischief as he sits beside me. 'I've got a motorcycle.'

'Seriously? Petrol?'

'Yes. One can still get it if one knows who to ask.'

'Scientist and an outlaw. I'm impressed. But how do you get about without being seen?'

'In the underground. The old rail system goes to the badlands. I fossick on my days off.'

'For what?'

'There's all kinds of interesting stuff left in Dodge. Like books and external hard drives with news broadcasts on them from before the crash.'

'And me.'

I sip my coffee and settle into the corner of his ratty but really comfy couch.

He turns and faces me, silly smirk on his face. 'Is that where you got caught?'

'Fell asleep pissed off my tits in an Irish pub call Raffertys. Bastard of a manager must've dobbed me in. Cowboys never would.'

'It was a bit silly going into a bar looking like a hybrid.'

'Sheesh, do I look that stupid? I was all woman when I went in. Musta fell asleep before the moon turned. Really dumb. I'm not fully stick insect till the dark of the moon.'

'What's with the moon?'

'Tidal. When the tide's out a gal like me—it's complicated. Pleasure'll get me killed one day. Really good hooch though.'

'I thought you were immortal?'

'Yeah, well I had a bottle to myself.'

'Moonshine?'

'Moonshine.'

'Not pretty dumb, hugely dumb.'

I punch him in the shoulder and sigh. 'I'll ask you later then.'

'About the batch?'

'Yeah. We better get away about now.'

He gets up, opens a chest of drawers here, a cupboard there and starts packing necessaries in a massive pair of panniers.

'Sit tight while I get organized.'

My carapace is dissolving back into my skin and my legs are fleshing out. 'You leaving anybody you love?'

He shuffles his feet then walks to the bed and drags a backpack from underneath.

'Not anymore. So, save it with the questions.'

He's about to stuff a T shirt and a rolled-up pair of jeans in with the rest. 'Can I have those,' I ask. 'Should come in useful any time now.' And he chucks them my way. I hold them with difficulty, but I hold them anyway.

4

Rumble

(Gamble)

IN THE BASEMENT IS A TRAPDOOR that lifts onto a concrete tube with a metal ladder descending into blackness.

'After you,' he says. He's brought a torch, so it isn't as spooky as it could have been.

The base is another two minutes away and I'm jelly-legged by the time I touch down on solid ground.

Terrence shines the beam of light up ahead and I'm speechless.

There it is. The stuff of legend. An ancient stripped-back and rebuilt Moto Guzzi Norge GT 8V complete with even more panniers, of real leather, and with super fat tires. Insane. I haven't seen one of them since back in the twenty first century. Terrence shoves his pack into one pannier and checks the other for equipment, pulls his belt from his jeans with a snap and reaches his arms behind my back.

'What're you doing,' I squeak.

'Tying your wings to your torso. We could ride rather fast. You'll suffer otherwise.'

He's so close I can smell him. I want to lick him, but I suppress the urge.

5

Empire

(Gamble)

THIS WHOLE NEW WORLD ORDER thing is an abysmal failure. There was just something so charming about soil, crooked teeth, wrinkles, pigeons and the stress of knowing there were termites in wooden houses and coughs that were actual illnesses rather than an excuse to gain attention.

When I'm all woman I keep my nipples taped down because I refuse the fashion trend of getting them removed. Because nipples have become offensive.

In the badlands it's all still there. It's okay to flash a bit of bosom and some people even allow hair on their bodies. It's still acceptable to be an atheist or agnostic or other Greek word for godless.

The world kind of fell to pieces back when the US dollar became a dirty word and Europe went into fiscal meltdown. It wasn't a far step to resurrect slavery to economic front and center. Shit, the whole of the west owed the Chinese its bright shiny title of Empire and it's never had a problem with that kind of labor, same as any other country.

6

Razorback

(Gamble)

THE MACHINE purrs and echoes its reverb onto the walls of the ancient storm water tunnel under a city that, once upon a time, was Tinseltown. Hollywood. Los Angeles, California. It's like a vibrator between my thighs but I hold on. Pretend to be chilled out when I'm so very, very close to orgasm I'm sweating and biting the sides of my tongue.

I prefer muck and monsters to sterile insecurity and phobia of the unknown and I ponder product legislation and a bit of consumer law-breaking (under-spending) to distract myself from lust and the

43

strain of wings in leathers as we rattle and roll along the towpath beside the tracks at…

I look over Terrence's shoulder and the base of my spine registers warning buzzes down my left leg. We're on ninety mile an hour. I'm not game to ask if he's crazy. Have I been saved only to line a half a mile of busted asphalt with my gore? Who drives this fast? Not nowadays anyways. Not with the concrete crumbling to non-existence. Never done speed of any kind, me. Well, that's a lie but it was so long ago it's pretty much theoretical.

The tunnel of blackness becomes a small spot of day in the far distance that swells exponentially onto the dawn of a scrubby desert the color of a waterlogged corpse.

We're okay now as long as we keep to the red rock and high cliffs as much as we can.

I know every cave and canyon, twisted spinifex and strangled gorge of this countryside like no one else and I give Terrence credit, he's taking navigation like a man.

Far below us are the threads of main arterials that crisscross the country like whip scars on a seditionist's back and they are crowded with, mainly, goat-drawn wagons—up to a quarter mile of the poor bastards, flogged by traders frightened of the prospect of being abroad come nightfall.

Badlands.

Every runaway slave or whore who refuses to lie on her back or non-believer with a big angry 666 branded onto their forehead or fuck-you-I-won't-do-what-you-tell-me artist. Every musician, poet, dreamer or shape-shifter out there learns to be a road thug just to make ends meet.

And I love them.

All of them micro-chipped, all able to have the wicked things surgically removed in Dodge. For a price. Most often allegiance.

There are incalculable traders and travelers on the arterial today as me and Terrence stop to chow down a picnic in the rich purple and orange shadow of the butte. So now I'm sated and no. No! Don't sleep now.

Then crash, bam, a thousand ancient freight trains rumbling through the caves of nightmare. I wake up and half the cliff is land sliding. And now I'm fully awake with rock crumbling and crashing down toward the road. Fire is out of control. People are screaming as they burn. Where earlier there was traffic there is now just an enormous sinkhole-looking maw in the ground and I thought the Mother had done her thing. But no. Road pirates have blown holes in the traders, not caring what gets fucked up as they ride out of the scrub below to take what they want.

We're not safe either and Terrence lifts me.

Then he drops me.

'Oh god!'

'What?' I wake fully, and I've got human legs and now I'm also on the ground so there's sand on my bum. I regain the jeans and T-shirt from where I'd placed them close to me just in case, and roughly cover myself.

'Stop staring, Terrence. We going, or what?'

He snaps up the kickstand and guns the engine. I straddle the pillion and hold onto him. With all my strength. I have come to realize that the man has no fear. And I thought I was the one in control.

We burn rubber along the Razorback.

'Yell if I need a different direction,' he calls over his shoulder.

'Keep straight.' Tears whip from my face by the hunger of a day ripped open by the bike and angry at our impudence.

Twilight greens across the parched sky as Dodge smudges the horizon. I dare a *phew*. But it's way too premature.

7

Tits and Head

(Gamble)

LATE AFTERNOON WE HIDE. ROCK deep. Snake country.

'Are you sure?' Terrence challenged when I'd yelled to pull over. 'What? Here?'

'Scorpions, tarantulas, rattlers, death adders, stuff like that but no men. So we're cool. Light a fire, I'll be back.'

All around is scattered with abundant wood from some long-dead forest and he begins collecting as I hightail into the scrub to set a few snares.

There're rabbits and rodents all over this piece of country and I surprise and crack the necks of two of the former in under an hour. Just as the sun oozes down below the horizon. Damn fine. I gut em, skin em and skewer em from mouth to bum and head back to camp. I set a Y in the ground at either end of Terrence's surprisingly well-made fire that has settled to high, hot coals, and set to turning our dinner.

The first bunny is done and, once fed, Terrence finally seems to relax. I'm sucking the marrow from the bones when he starts with the questions.

'So. My little winged friend. Again. What are you?'

I swallow some lumpy obstruction, probably the prospect of his reaction, before I can speak. 'I'm part of the spirit world.'

You could have cut the deep twilight with a spoon for a good thirty seconds.

'You're having me on.'

'Do you want me to tell you?'

'You might as well,' he smiles. A look in his eyes.

I punch him on the shoulder like before and hope the bruise is starting to get good and lurid by now. He hugs his knees, grinning into the fire. He's enjoying baiting me.

'I'm a manifestation of the spirit world and like I already told you I used to be the rock of ragged, jagged islands way off the coast of Ireland back before monks moved in. Being stone was just too slow and out there in the ocean like that, was way too isolated. I've never been proficient with patience.'

He actually snorts back a laugh. I wait for him to explain himself before I continue.

'Sorry. Ready. Do continue.'

'And in the spirit world there's the Grace. You know of this?'

'No. And if this is some incredibly imaginative psychotic episode I'll be able to tell, you know. I'm watching your pupils. They dilate when you lie, you realize.'

I lean right up in front of his face, eyes wide open. 'Go ahead and stare, lover boy.'

He tries not to, but he drops his gaze first. Scuffs his boots in the dust. Mere mortal indeed.

Then the ground shudders. But not with earthquake. Louder. Staccato. We both stand and peer into the sea of night with what looks like a dust cloud coming towards us at speed.

Then one hundred, two hundred, a thousand horses flood out of the blackness and fork in two as they approach our fire. Terrence is terrified and crouches behind the Guzzi. As if that could protect him. But they power on past us and within seconds are gone.

'Wow!' gasps Terrence when he can get the words out. 'Were they mustangs?! Thank god. We still have mustangs!'

'They're not wild horses, Terrence.'

'Of *course* they're wild. We… we could have been killed.'

'Finish your dinner.' I'm nonchalant. Don't want him working too much out till I can get him where I need him.

'Look at you. You're hiding something, Gamble. You *know* about what just happened.'

I shrug and sit back down, my wings about the last thing to change back. I spread my legs and expose my bare feet to the fire because feeling the cold is a human thing.

Terrence joins me, squatting, gulping back half a flask of water.

'Are you going to tell me?' he squints. 'You weren't surprised at all.'

'Can I finish telling you my story?'

'Och, you might as well. You'll not explain about what just happened, will you? And is that still alright to eat, do you think?' He indicates the last of the bunnies. 'Really peculiar events make my blood sugar go silly.'

'Shall I continue?'

He's jiggling the skewer from hand to hand to stop it burning him. 'You want some?'

'No, I don't want anything except to finish answering your fucking original question.'

He sinks his teeth into the flesh, grunts with pleasure and gestures a pathetically patronizing hand in my direction. I could bite it off, but he saved me, so I'll give a little.

'The Grace. She's life. Is everything. So I, being I, I called out to her. Begged that I be allowed to be some other piece of the world. She said I was being obscure, so I thought about it. For two hundred years or thereabouts. Finally I had it but it was complicated.'

'So, is this Grace some sort of genius loci? A goddess? You keep referring to her as a she. And I'm not for one moment taking the piss, mind you, but she grants wishes to rocks? You can hear how this sounds, Gamble.'

He chucks the last of the bones onto the coals.

'Then I knew what I wanted to be, Terrence.'

'Let me guess—'

I ignore him. 'A stick insect—a praying mantis, actually—gets to chew the head off its mate when the sex is done was one, and well-endowed human woman, the other.

'And you don't seem to be doing either well, at all.'

'Shut up, Terrence. Let me finish.'

'Sorry…'

'*You got it*, the Grace had said. *But you have to agree to the consequences.* I'd asked what they were but she's fickle like that and just up and turned into a thunderstorm.'

'You intending to bite my head off?' squirms Terrence.

'Nup.'

'Thank you.'

'We haven't had sex yet.'

'And we're not going to,' he puffs up, horrified.

I smile.

8

Rhino

(Gamble)

WE DEFY THE ROUGH TRACK, TEARING up dust and sand so even the bright, new moon looks like blood. It's just before dawn in that strange pale half-light, and the wind's biting the flesh of my naked arms like fire ants, when the roar of somewhere like a hundred, high powered, heavy metal armored militia vehicles drive straight towards us from the stark but obvious distraction, to an otherwise pointless and barren horizon that is Dodge. The rhino—a demilitarized tank—is at the front of the pack. It turns its high beam on us as Terrence twists the bike off the track in an utterly useless attempt at escape.

The militia is scaring the shit outa Terrence along with my tits pushing against his back like children vying for attention. The bike skids and we land in a pool of mud that once would have called itself a lake, pinned within the spotlight of the leader of the pack.

'That you, Gamble?'

The hatch of the rhino flips open and Alice climbs out of the turret and onto the hull, throws his arms into the air like he's at the roller derby and we're winning. Oblivious to the chill he's naked to the waist and wearing a McLeod tartan kilt with hand-tooled leather boots—the ones with the spurs. He jumps down into the dust, thrusts a hip to the side and makes his guns in his belt more stable.

'And you've brought me a kitten,' he grins, eyeing Terrence.

'Garment,' I demand. 'I'm feeling human.'

'Chuck us something will ya, Rottie?' Alice calls down to the gunner inside, and a big ex-army greatcoat sails through the air from the hatch like a vengeful flat old soldier. I grab it before it lands and wrap it around myself.

'Terrence, this is Alice. And Alice is that a gun in your pocket or are you just pleased to see me?'

'Oh, the cliché!' He grins and scarpers back up the side of the truck.

'We're on food. You comin or headin into the hills?

'Meet you back at the compound.'

'Oh, and Terrence...'

'Yes?'

'Just because I'm glamorous doesn't make me a pushover.'

'I'm sorry?'

'You got the look of a genome dealer.'

'A… A what?'

Alice pulls a cigar and a Zippo from his sporran, nips the end of the stogie with his teeth and lights it, billowing blue smoke into the dawn wind. Rottie pops his shaggy head of dirty blond curls above the port hole to have a gander. He smiles. Alice pushes him back inside and prepares to drop the hatch.

'We'll talk later, Gamble. You know I don't like surprises.' All serious and threat.

The convoy grinds off like a protest march of grumpy old men and I amble back to Terrence whose mouth is still open.

'Who on earth are all those people?'

'Just get on the fucking bike, Terrence. I'll explain when we get to Constance.'

'What?'

'It's a town.'

'Oh.'

9

Badlands

(Gamble)

CANYONS. VALLEYS. THE ECHO of water gushing somewhere. Otherwise mile upon barren mile.

'I'm running out of gas, Gamble,' Terrence yells, his spit dusting my cheek in an unconsciously intimate way.

'Eyes ahead, lover.'

Up on the buttes. Sentries. Semi-automatic machine guns over a shoulder here, bows and quivers of arrows there. Some savage looking fuckers done up in war paint and cammos. No mucking about. I know what they're doing. They're letting us in. Like guard dogs. Let em in, then bail em up against the wall carrying an armload of thievery.

We round a bend and there it is. Used to be a mining hub. Now it belongs to a chieftain named Mukata. Old tohunga. Shape-shifter. Ruru being her totem and all. Full moko tapped into her chin no one knows how long ago, and the word *Justify* inked into her neck in letters writ large enough for there to be no mistaking. Took to the whare wānanga her mother had taught her in secret and can seriously use that magic when she needs it. Predicting acid rain, drones, the big, unsummoned djinn storms that'll kill you faster than a nuclear meltdown in your kitchen, raiders and pirates and police. She hasn't got it wrong once. Even told me the gin'd get me in trouble one day. Did I listen? No. Who listens to old people, was my line of thinking. Hence, I prepare for her disdain as we cruise on into town.

She's sitting on her porch smoking that little Dutch pipe one of her students dredged up from the old city. Maybe ninety kilograms of solid muscle. Face and body of nut brown chamois leather crinkled into folds like a landscape. Her one blind eye is milky-white, but it sees into the blood of a thousand, thousand ripped up, chain-saw-massacred forests. And every fucking one of those trees knew her as mother. She's given birth to a dying earth, but it hasn't stripped her of one specter of wildness.

She's got talismans in small skin pouches around her neck and a straight back that's had the skin flayed off it so often it's like a railroad shunting yard. She said, when I turned up, 'We had us a piece of what modern day people called Ireland turn up in Waitangi oh, back in the 1800s. Took to one of our men and bore him two children. Strong-willed woman. She was about when the English wanted us all historically rewritten, so I can smell you.'

'You can?' I'd said.

'Yes, and yer fatally fucking flawed deal with the Grace.'

And I love her like a mother.

She smokes wormwood. She also smokes the occasional cane toad as well. When she can get it.

We pull up and I hop off. Terrence kills the engine, snaps out the kickstand. Pockets the keys just in case. We walk the few steps it takes to get to the porch. I stop to stroke the flank of Paint's massive horse that's tied loosely to the hitching post and that turns his head towards me with a whuffle of recognition.

'Jesus, you're a dumb cunt sometimes Gamble,' says Mukata, standing. 'So, you brought the enemy right to us. Get him inside.'

'I'm not...' begins Terrence.

'Te tangata, I'm not listening and not saying a fucking word until we find out if you light up, eh?'

'What are you saying?' Terrence asks politely.

59

'Oops,' I say.

'What?!' Terrence yells.

'Sorry,' is all I have to offer right now.

Two cowpoke that've been sitting like bookends at the edges of the top step, idle down. They join us silently. Paint is six six and as black as the inside of a safe, with piercings and body-mods all over his face and chest. He's got the mottles of a pinto, like wine stains, attesting to his own animal blood. Won't smile no matter what. Understand. His human people were almost wiped out on the Trail of Tears, the horses that make up much of his true nature dwindling almost to extinction. Till he and the other warriors saved them.

We all get him. Justice can torture a refugee in his or her own country.

The other is Ragtime. True lady. Thin as a ripped lizard. That might cause a stranger to think she had an eating disorder. But the muscle corded under that flawless porcelain Japanese flesh can wield a blade-edged fan like a sensei. Terrence sighs at me as I shrug the greatcoat deeper onto my body and they escort him into the house after Mukata, me following, a chastised stray.

Inside is like the Mad Hatter's lab. Mukata likes to play around with mind-altering substances. She tries them out herself first, I must admit. It's all old magic meant to close up the blind spot people got in their heads that doesn't allow communication with animals and trees and such.

Like a rogue gene.

Splitting us humans into two separate two-legged animals. The half that aren't us—the mad bastards—are the species in control of Wonderland and the big pharma labs. Silicon Valley.

Same one's as keep on creating hybrids and those poor wee transdroids.

The ones they haven't euthanized and incinerated in those big ovens, or imprisoned just in case.

Whatever's easiest.

They don't think other species got feelings.

Think they don't experience pain.

The screaming is some automatic nerve response, same as when the butcher cuts the head off the chickens, and it keeping him entertained by running around for hours after.

Mukata's had my back for a long time. Accepting of my careless foibles. And there's this plan. But I'll get to that. In the meantime, they have Terrence. We follow them inside.

'I'm not packing,' Terrence whispers as they drag him to the bench. 'Seriously. I took care of it.' No good. No one's asking him to explain. No one trusts him anywhere near yet. There he is under the laser getting scanned for the mote-sized device. It could take a while so Mukata and I go sit on the porch now the sun's up and she sighs, pulling out her pouch of wormwood, tamping down her pipe and lighting it, offering it first to the day before sucking back a drag. She turns towards me with her good eye just as the last of my wings slide beneath the skin flap along either side of my latissimus dorsi, then closes, with her never even blinking.

'Little Earth, doesn't matter what *you* are,' she starts off, 'you're getting sloppy and if he's missed already, and you're in the surveillance. Are you in the surveillance? Of *course* you are in the surveillance. The drones'll be hunting.'

'But they only saw what they thought was a hybrid, they wouldn't recognize me anyway.'

'And they wouldn't have seen your little mate carrying you away? So, no one's gonna miss him?'

But she's interrupted. The door to the lab pulled open.

'He wasn't lying,' says Ragtime, boots scuffing against the welcome mat, Paint behind her leaning on the door frame.

'What's that about?' Mukata's brow hardly ever scrunches but this has her perplexed.

'He's microchipped but it's just info. There's no tracker,' Ragtime adjusts the two katanas in her obi.

'Hmm. That's a first and a bit of a mystery. But not for now. We have an appointment to parlay with the chiefs about what setting the plan in motion. Paint, can you get us the horses?'

'Sure.' His voice is like soft and sonorous as he pulls the reins free.

'Thanks Paint. Kia marino horapa huri noa koutou.

'Back as soon as I can.'

'Oh,' Ragtime sits spread-legged on the bottom step, as Paint mounts his massive horse and canters down the street towards the end of town. 'One other thing…'

'Well?' asks Mukata.

'Terrence reckons he's got a crew of his own. If we need them.'

'What have you brought me, Gamble?'

I squirm.

Whuria te tangata
Weave the people together

10

Genius

(Terrence)

OH, THE THEORETICAL KNOWLEDGE OF the genome. I say theoretical because I came to the realization, even as a young boy, that humanity is adventuring with quirky but terrible ideas. Based on curiosity. I know that. Like God as a name and not a concept. Oh, as an aside, I know when I use the ridiculous terms like god and christ and all that old religious wankery but they're wired in. Bloody good expletives. I know I'm saying them but it's like comfort food.

Where was I? Och, aye. People built barriers of war around the sciences to protect them from people who use the same word/name to build yet other walls. How far back does that go into known territory? Jericho? Deeper? History has never been my strong forte, so I'm scanty at the best of times. But I was always going to end up in scientific research. It's a very, very safe discipline in these times. The literature speculates that our primary relatives on planet earth are bacteria living around undersea hydrothermic vents. I was taught that one such bacterial split happened about 15.6 million years ago when the gorilla lineage diverged from the other hominids. The other bacterial split happened about 5.3 million years ago the time our more human lineage separated from that of bonobos.

Me? My heritage is guilt ... or a possible inherited propensity towards mindless cruelty.

I have not known the second of these yet and I sometimes contemplate what could possibly trigger it into manifestation. But I can't imagine. I could just be a shitty little man-boy speculating that the work in genetics enhancement sciences is benign, when, in reality, I am utterly aware that it is profoundly brutal, thoughtless, sterile, clinical and heartless.

I come from a long line of lairds and my family has traced our ancestors back to Norman MacLeod, the prick that left us indebted. He had his first wife disposed of in a dungeon and left to starve. A man who also had the tenants that farmed the lands thereabouts, the *Sgiathanach*, shipped to the new colonies as slaves. I'm so embarrassed.

My grandfather acquired a traveling carnival. Something nostalgic to do with his childhood, I suppose. He and his management team bought and sold people and animals with whimsy I was born and raised on the road as was my own father. He hated it. My mother was a punter at their penny and dime show (they'd sold off the elephant and both tigers by then) in the dustbowl years and they fell in love at first sight.

She was loaded, turns out. Her dad was a mogul who engineered gas pipelines, and yes, she was slumming with the carnies. But one look into my father's soulful blue Celtic eyes and she was already married. I was their only child due to the Empire's reintroduced one-child policy.

The theatre, over a hundred years old when they bought her, had been a joint labor of love. They restored her and showed old art house movies on her silver screen. I was in university when the flu hit, killing most everybody outside Wonderland. Including them.

Way back in little school we children had been taught that the entire continent, beyond the domes, was unlivable. Endless toxic miles of dust and carnage. Minefields of disease and famine. A rusted, busted up, polluted soup of radiation and carbon emissions. That if any people still survived out there they would be barbaric in every way we could imagine. Only snakes and toads and lizards and spiders left to hunt. And each other. So said the propaganda. Lies, of course.

Wonderland is safe. All plastic and light. The highest quality lab facility outside of China. Silicon Valley, body-mods, cocaine and style. With pristine pumped air. Of course, there is still the quaint antique architecture allowed for nostalgia. Like my theatre and the Slums of Sunset Strip, Bacon Street and the like. Enough vendors of anything and everything to make nightlife-whimsy good sport. Brothels are more lucrative than ever, and Chinese owned and operated opium dens abound for the right cred. I rather speculate that it's revenge. But then most people forget most things and have no idea about the Opium Wars four hundred years ago this year. I'll always remember something as interesting as that. I have an eidetic memory. It's an intergenerational curse.

Both Wonderland and the Slums support countless backroom deals for connoisseurs of mutants, blood diamonds, abortions, the buying and selling of children for servitude and pretty little transdroids as sex slaves and for private collections. These are people I despise, gambling more money than I'll see in my lifetime on dogfights and to-the-death with bare knuckles. An entertainment industry that also includes politics because people got savvy a hundred years ago that governments have nothing to do with running a country and everything to do with being a front for the international people trade. It was the government that began the herding, selling and disposing of vulnerable and impoverished people. With no one game enough to try to stop them. They had money and a mandate. And the media.

Enough propaganda was fabricated to present the sad, mentally ill and financially depleted within our societies; parasitic. A burden to a suffering economy that had really been buggered ages beforehand. It's all about supply and demand really. And let's face it, we couldn't keep them.

We'd rid ourselves of manufacturing over a hundred years ago so what were all those people being born going to do? Business, as I skimmed over earlier, is run by private sector bejeweled, security-guarded thugs now, the money going into the coffers of the new empire.

That's the spin. When the flu became a pandemic just a few years ago those not cashed up died. There were only two working antibiotics left in the world and they were worth more than a fugu itamae. Dead at the first sneeze.

My mother had visited a fortune teller when I was still a little boy. The old woman mapped out the dismals of the future and warned Mummy to get me into the sciences or else.

I'm a bit of a genius. I'm not flaunting it. It got me through university by the time I was sixteen. I completed an eight year science degree in four, specializing in biodiversity genetics. The plague. I was snapped up by Xin Oro International when the final pandemic raged. I was behind locked and sterile laboratory doors, working to pay off an eternally impossible university debt. Within two weeks those who were going to die were dead. The big money was spent on the cleanup. No estimates, still, on how many had perished. No one asked, and no one said. That was eight years ago.

The entertainment industry ran out of Marvel remakes and had to discover a way of keeping people distracted from their predicaments, so they joined forces with the health industry.

In a kismet twist of mutuality porn also became passé. Nobody is shocked anymore and for a goodly decade hetero-men got to the point that they couldn't get their dicks up around real women anyway because their neurons were wired to jerking off at a screen. Also, because of the endemic spread of 21st century plastics, sperm is worth more than uranium and almost non-existent. Blokes with good swimmers hide behind mansion walls bristling with security because semen sells for a small fortune. I have utterly no idea if mine works at all. Should I ever have sex with a willing woman I might find out.

The rapid decline in western society-style babies caused a huge rise in snake-oil cures for everything. Conservation and Wildlife Tourism was born and that's where genetic mutations and hybridization came into their heyday. Not anyone living hadn't seen a wildlife documentary about mostly extinct species and everybody knew what a farm animal looked like, so what else was there to keep successful people happy and quiet?

Created in the labs and grown to maturity in specially designed pens: carnivorous pelicans. Hairless bears. Dogs small enough to keep on a keychain. Rats the size of goats. The latter are terrific because they became a kitch and funky protein source (once the flea problem was eradicated) that does not require antibiotics to fatten them. They are all white of course. No one wants to eat as colored rat. Chickens are bred potted like yoghurt, without bones or offal.

We created species. At first only other animals because we still didn't think of ourselves as such. Then, back in twenty-one twenty, the false ethics of it all crumbled for good.

Big pharma grew pig people; glow in the dark pig people. This was a huge success on two fronts. Firstly, they became the newest form of food for other species, bred to feed us, and secondly, hugely entertaining because there was something about the eyes. Something distinctly human that mesmerized observers. Almost as if there was someone like us actually in there. That's when the idea of hybrid zoos became viable.

Have I mentioned that jobless and homeless people were corralled? Them and anyone with a disability or mental illness. Herded onto reservations? Organ harvesting was the first reason. *Welfare costs the taxpayer...* We all knew the spin. You were there. You would have heard it. Possibly even agreed to the policy. One had to protect oneself and one's own interests or risk joining them.

Then the enforced surrogacy of human children for purchase by childless couples was introduced. Not that this is anything new. Child trafficking is as old as Herod. Now stem cells from cord blood and aborted fetuses. Longevity and athleticism from human colostrum. The specialized breeding of designer babies. Then we bred even more successfully incubated new species. Hybrids are grown in the wombs of women and purpose-bred captive great apes. These females are

71

segregated from the general population because...well...because of shame, really. That of their creators.

For years I'd been a secret hunter. I didn't know what I was hunting for, but I knew I'd know when I found it. I discovered long-abandoned railways. I followed the tracks as far as I could, in whatever time I could and four years ago I struck it lucky. One of the lines lead me to a vast, abandoned something. What? A small city? It's hard to explain really. The complex housed shops with nothing remaining in most. Oh, shelves moldered in some; some held decaying stainless-steel racks. In others naked mannequins looked like spooky plastic people. Empty steel frames wide open to the elements, the shattered glass of windows a snowfield across the expanse of flooring. Outside antiquated, dilapidated aircraft, rusted into dereliction, across a tarmac of dead grass and broken bitumen.

Some corridors led underground by way of corrugated stairway, so black that they almost ate my torchlight. Down there were countless, forever-locked doorways that once guided passengers to air transport across the world with ease.

I explored vast concrete tunnels and it was in one of these that I discovered the service bay from which I scored my bike. Covered in greasy dust and cobwebs as she was, I'd pushed her through the night, to the bay down by the dead sea. Into a storm water outlet where, deep inside, I left her until I could access the old city. The records at the

Metropolitan Board of Works found the ordinance maps. I studied every twist and turn. Because there was a grill in the alley out back of my theatre and yes, of course I explored inside. The ladder drops down sixty feet, the storm water tunnel dry, all the way to the oily, brackish shoreline.

And that's where I encountered the first of the free people—rebels—one black and moonless night.

They were what we call *cleanskins*. Neither had ever been jabbed. Bull and Rattlesnake Lil. They aided runaway hybrids to freedom. They are people smugglers. And the twenty-two refugees of that particular night had all escaped from one of the vast network of reservations together. They huddled, like newborn kittens in the dark, waiting for the boat to sail them north along the coast, to some country I did not know of. I thought I would die when both the big man and his savage little flower of a partner charged me. After a long and tearful begging session they agreed to take me hostage until I could be enlisted.

'What border?' I'd asked, later, when I'd been accepted. It was the first I'd ever heard of the legend of the northern lands.

Rattlesnake sighed, and explained that way up top of the continent there's a border. This side of the river is owned by China and her allies: the droid factories, the McDonalds franchises of www-dot-meat-dot-com, the laboratories creating and harvesting organs for proper people and for the food that their cattle are fed. Worldwide Pharma production and Silicon Valley's build and reboot robotics facilities, droid and cyborg construction and maintenance, and the royalty that upholds the capital of these enterprises for the empire. The other side was, though, probably quite primitive compared even to the Slums because the people there apparently live in forests.

They think.

Truth is, Bull and Rattlesnake could have been dealing with smugglers killing off the runaways just as soon as they sailed into the deep dead water. Dumping them in that sewage and plastic swamp. Who'd know? I never asked where they'd met the sailors, or found out about them in the first place.

It was through them and the education they provided that I, hence, was made aware of the extent of the atrocities to which I was an unwitting accomplice. And well, because I joined them. I became an outlaw. It's in my nature.

11

The Slums

(Terrence)

BULL'S, WELL, BULL'S CALLED BULL BECAUSE he's that big. His mother became pregnant with him outside the allotted breeding program for women of color. She had to disappear. She hid within the labyrinth of back alleys and kept a low profile, but other hideaways took notice. Word on the street reached her that 21 Ramsay Street, a bakery to all extents and purposes, was a front for women in dire straits; to ask for Mme. Jolis. Five months later the elderly French midwife delivered an eleven kilogram baby boy.

Bull's mother died when he was still a lad and he ran away and joined the rodeo circuit. He started out learning the clown trade but then Early Lewis came along, first black man to ride and to win. He taught Bull everything he could. Early had AIDS and didn't know how long before the antivirals stopped his decline. Bull was to be his *fuck-you* legacy to the white aristocracy of the gladiator sport. He went from winning to owning, after one too many spectacles of cruelty. He earned enough money to invest in a best of breed Wagyu, obsidian black, named Midnight Express. Bill sold the stud's semen for 28,000 creds a straw, for a year. Early, still alive, bought up-country where there's still some good grazing. And several pretty Wagyu ladies. Bull gave his mentor the stud when he retired. A gift of honor. When he bought his Airstream trailer he also named it Midnight Express. He decked it out as a bar and performance venue. Now, at twenty-nine he's a proud black independent businessman, his clothing hand-made in Little Shanghai Town by the sons of ancient tailors, his crisp white shirts painstakingly pressed, the bling of his jewelry the real deal.

Three years ago Bull fell in love with Rattlesnake Lil. They became partners in the running of the bar with Lil taking bookings months ahead for the performers. She laid a hoodoo of confusion over the trailer so that only patrons could recognize it. She's as lean as… what do they say? As lean as she can be mean. Her mother is Chinese, but her father is unknown, but obviously she'd been slumming with some Anglo boy. As long as a woman's matrilineal lineage is high-born who she fucks is up to her.

Lil's mother was trained by her own mother as a *wuyu*. That's a sorceress and that hoodoo has got gristle. Lil grew up in the club scene and, backstage, after ordinary classes in exotic dance and sexual acumen, her mother educated her in the ancient lineage of spell-casting and the making of poisons. She also learned about profit and loss, the economics of communist capitalism and blue-chip investment.

Her mind is like a poker player, however, meaning she doesn't show this aspect of herself to anyone other than Bull. She makes the most of mother orient by dressing in skin-tight red silk and retro Doc Martens with those little silver razor blades set into the toes. They call her after the rattlesnake for that ring she wears on the little finger of her left hand. Filigree stainless steel and inset with diamonds, it's shaped to a needle point. Has she ever used it? She raised her pencil thin eyebrows without looking up from the cocktail she was mixing when I asked. I never asked again.

The Midnight Express is a gleaming chrome Airstream trailer. Preferred venue of artists, poets, political dissidents and rock-n-rollers. From beers to ketamin cocktails, snacks of barbequed rodent, pizza replacement jellies and corn on the cob without the butter, to top shelf black market opiates. Even has a jukebox that still plays the classics from the Age of Enlightenment. *Metallica. Guns n Roses. Pink.* The trailer moves from one low street to another to avoid predictability. Best way to get stung, be predictable. They have the networks covered so their regulars always know where to find them.

Basin Street. Ramsay Street. Sunset Boulevard. Down where the big freighters used to dock before the waters rose and swamped it. Where the nuke subs unloaded their dirty waste, and shipped it cross country in long convoys. That rather horrid little event occurred at night; dumped on indigenous land because no one ever upheld the treaties.

The old city is known as the Slums. It is a'strut with hookers and white boys from Wonderland where there are dealers of everything that could either give a woman ecstasy or kill a man for a couple of shillings worth of cred.

Police cruise in bullet-proof black and whites, as well as on foot in pairs. Dressed to kill in balaclavas and Kevlar, toting semi-automatics and attitude, eyes and ears alert for the homeless or people so off their chops that without a bar code, identity implant or other legitimate outer-dome visa they're destined for detention. It's just a jump to the left from there to the reservations. The end of them.

Paper books are available to the elite as these things are as rare as clean underwear, and the makers of musical instruments and dream-catchers do better than the fire dancers or the young, half naked women on stilts. The police don't even arrest the performers in the labia display show. I'm quite chuffed at the lady who earns a few quid artistically displaying untrimmed, unwaxed genitals. It's educational.

I was relaxing in the bar at the Midnight Express one night, nursing a Defender, straight up no ice, when a mainly human hybrid with just a touch of something reindeer (by the smell of him), saunters by me, sporting a black Stetson pulled down low over his eyes. He sets up his stool at the end of the trailer amidst the twinkle and glimmer of multi-colored party lights. He opens an actual leather case and brings out a Fender, a priceless steel-string guitar, at least a hundred years old. No one's game to ask where he stole it. Not in here. He's all in black and not a smile for anyone. Long ice white hair in two braids, his skin inked everywhere visible, silver rings on his fingers and turquoise at his ears. And no, he's not supposed to be here but every runaway hybrid hiding out in the Slums knows the place. He plugs in his amp, slides the glass tube onto his middle finger and fires up a slow riff. I ought to have known he'd be a classicist. He riffs of a few bars of blues, in what's obviously his own style, before he ices the crowd with *I Went Down to St James Infirmary*. I was blissfully transported to my grandfather's study, his pride being the deck with the diamond stylus and the box full of vinyl.

Then wham, zing, fuck me, old fellow! I know I've been drugged. I sprawl across the bar towards Lil, mouthing *Now?* And I hear, like from the end of a long dark tunnel, *Surprise, surprise.*

I awoke in some sealed off facility with fluffy walls. In case I needed to bounce off them? Swathed in bandages. Burned. I knew it'd be bad, but it was quite fine really because the drugs weren't, and I

79

know the identi-trace has been lasered out of me. I am a free man. My entry level identi-chip implant is the highest security access a scientist can get so no one will think to bother checking my blood.

'R'you in there, Terrence?' It's Bull. He's holding a cup of java. I can smell it. 'Wakey wakey.'

I sit up. It's more difficult than I thought it was going to be.

'Where are we?'

'We're in an old maximum-security psych incubator. No one to hear you scream, son. No burning smell to pick up. Here, drink this.'

I take the cup of the thickest blackest most bitter coffee available and I sip.

'Welcome to the Underground Railway.' He smiles back over his shoulder as he heads to the door. 'When you feel better we'll be out in the gardens. The rhododendrons still bloom here. Beautiful.'

So, my inclusion in this insurrection was now official. That propensity towards cruelty I was always afraid of? It was never going to manifest. I'm a person of extreme empathy. I smiled. I'd been given the night off anyway. Go fuck something I was told. Go fuck something! Then I laughed. This was better than nitrous.

12

The Lab

(Gamble)

'HOW LONG DO I HAVE TO STAY in here?' grumbles Terrence.

'Till the powwow's over and the chiefs decide whether we execute the plan now, rather than later.'

'You're being obscure, and I feel like a prisoner when all I've done is been your liberator and a sounding board for your constant chatter. What plan?'

'Sorry. Can't go into that. Not my place. Here. Can you scratch me just between my shoulders? My wings get dried outa here, even under the skin. I think it's old age.'

'Och, Jesus.'

But he does, and it feels so wonderful that I lean back into him, rubbing my hand against the front of his jeans. He, being he, jerks back and fumbles for his shot glass.

'You are a very bad insect, Gamble. That is not going to happen. Ever.'

'Are you blushing? You are!'

He tries so hard to appear offended that I laugh out loud.

'Oh Terrence, I'm immortal. I don't do good and bad. They're rubbish. Whoever invented them shoulda been slapped.'

'You think so, do you?' Terrence paces, gagging just a little when he downs the moonshine. 'You're all jolly with bounty hunters bagging and boxing you like that?'

'You were never going to euthanize me, were you?'

I sashay over to him and shove him down on one of the chairs, sit on his lap facing him. 'And I shoulda known that as soon as I saw you. Fuckers don't know about grooming and style. Here, let me take your mind off your jail.'

I lean into him and run my fingers through his hair, press my heaving breasts into his chest and position my lips as close to his, without actually kissing him, as I can. Just for the tease.

I lose the big coat.

'You're a predator,' he whispers.

'Yes, I am, Terrence.'

I tear off the T shirt.

He leans away from me just long enough to pull off his own. I undo his belt and jag down his zipper.

'We won't be alone for long,' he whispers hoarsely.

'Long enough, lover boy,' I reply, smooth as mercury.

I drop my jeans down and slide them off one foot, mounting him like I'm straddling his motorcycle.

'Don't you dare change,' he breathes raggedly. I laugh. I get the implication. Then his fingers dabble into all my moist horny places, transforming the joke to a moan, a smile of delight, then, oh my, the howl of a vixen but quietly, just in case anybody's in earshot.

I'm not that brassy.

(Paint)

Peculiar weather, earlier today, as I rode up onto the buttes and into the caves where the vast majority of elders live. In traditional ways. Remembering the songs and stories, the old skills to teach the children who have been kept safe from the factories and the reservations. Free people for the time being.

Above us the sky was dark with green cloud. All afternoon. We've had no rain in a decade but sure looked like we was in for a whole lot of just that. Forked lightning for well on an hour. Then a short while back afore sunset as we rode into Constance the whole lot just misted away. But we're all waiting for something. Ozone is thick in the air and the hairs are standing up on my forearms. I'm as old as this land and the native horses that run here once, and that do so again now.

I whistled the herd back here last night because of the drones. Army gets wind of them there'll be a war.

Years ago, we rustled them from where the palefaces had the last of the species imprisoned for slaughter. Lost a couple of thousand warriors in that run. No matter. We're all back from the brink of extinction. That does matter. Ain't no one not hill-born going to find us or them. I'm just pondering this when the ground lurches and things go crash bang. Medium-sized earthquake rattling all the glass everything inside. Everybody, except those two in there makin love, move outside just in case. Because the earth has been really quiet for a long time now and it's an ominous sign. The off-the-Richter-scale-demolition-big-one has been predicted for years, but that so far has not come.

Earlier today we sat around the fire for hours. A hundred and seventy-two elders of the tribes of every country. In the end it was decided that Mukata could exercise the freedom run whenever she please. She said that's about now so everyone's up on how furry the trouble could get real soon and they're preparing. Mukata went with them when they went back up country. Making magic with them. I'm back hanging out with Ragtime, just smoking on the porch of the lab, listening to the two inside doing what comes natural, despite what she is.

Then another grumble but this time it's the convoy.

Ragtime *ninjas* up onto the railing, and from there onto the roof, to watch for their dust. Rottie's her sweetheart and she gets spooked every time him and Alice and the band of brothers heads out to the old city. She wouldn't mind if she was with them. She's not afraid of dying and never has been. But people disappear. Often. It's like they never were and that's the cruelty she fears. The never knowing thing. She's needed here in Constance with me though.

Rotti parks the rhino and Alice jumps down. Two explosions of dust as his boots stomp what had grown grass once upon a time.

'Mukata?!' Mukata!'

Rotti rolls out of the confines of the hatch and slides into Ragtime's fierce hug.

'Where the fuck's the Mother, Raggers?'

Alice has to be patient a bit though. Kissing comes afore information in Ragtime's world. So, the former heads towards the lab, and through the door, without knocking, and I follow. Got to love a good show, dammit.

I follow Alice into the lab.

'Goodness me,' Alice groans at seeing Gamble and Terrence so disposed. Rolling his eyes. Not backing out but looking the other way. I smile so no one can see. Love's love so they don't bother me one iota. We boot across the room: past them, the equipment, the dubious contents in vats and obvious ones floating in formaldehyde in the transparent ones. Towards the kitchen area, and the Kooka along the far wall. In need of a strong cup of tea.

'You drink tea, chief?' asks Alice, pausing spooning the loose-leaf contraband into the pot.

'Not your best kilt, Alice,' calls Gamble over Terrence's shoulder, between grunts.

'Taunt me all you like, Little Earth, your squeeze there has shook up a hornet's nest. But that aside, I'm a lady and hence I'm fucken polite, so either a you two want a cuppa?'

(Gamble)

Interrupting me when I'm right at the sticky end of the wedge is like trying to pull two dogs apart in a brawl and there not being a hose within a hundred miles. If there did happen to be a conflagration in town it'd be fucked. All things considered Alice just fills the blackened kettle and settles it on the heat to boil and walks back outside.

I was done a while back, but Terrence just keeps on going. Who'd have thought? He looks so... What? Like a puppy. Then one mad, exotic, pupil-dilated groan and he's right where he should be. Then such a look crosses his face, the wonder in his eyes as he lifts his chin towards me and kisses me. Hey, crazy skellig woman. Don't fall for that look. You could drown if you're not careful. So I back off. I can't love. No way. That shit's way too scary. Tried it once. He got old and turned to dust and that was the worst day of my eternal fucking life.

I hop off and pull up the jeans. Tug on the boots I'd left behind here last time, and straighten up in general.

'Outside, soldier,' I say, hoisting Terrence to his feet and zipping him. He's grinning. *Stop that.*

'We miss anything?' I ask Paint who's following Alice outside.

'Nah. You're good,' he smiles, his dark mottles looking more scarlet than usual. I go out with the big boys, leaving Terrence to do whatever he has to.

'Mukata!' Alice yells to the air.

'She went back with the other elders. Making arrows and ware wānanga,' says Ragtime, hefting her semi onto her shoulder and adjusting the lay of the daisho now strapped to her back. 'Reckons guns're too noisy and that we'll all be fucked when we run outa bullets anyway. She'll be on her way.'

Terrence sits on the top step and pulls me down beside him. Puts his arm around me fer fuck' sake.

'Kettle's boiling,' he says to Paint.

I remove Terrence's arm and lean on the wood in the opposite direction. Bit of sex and he thinks we're an item? Good Grace.

'There's drones out all over the badlands,' says Alice lighting a cigar and jabbing his finger towards us two. 'They'll be looking for you is my guess.'

'Please,' Terrence sighs in frustration, 'everyone, my friends in the Slums can help. If you'll just let me explain.'

Paint's whistle is almost the pitch that breaks eardrums but people, dogs, horses, camels, hybrids and mutants come from every which way. Wherever they been holed up.

Mukata, bareback astride a piebald shire horse, canters into town with a bunch of native folk from all over everywhere. She dismounts beside Terrence.

'We need to conclude our conversation, Terrence. And we need to parlay with those friends of yours with the magic bus.'

'Finally,' he mutters. 'Um… hang about. I haven't had a chance to tell you about them so how–'

'You think I haven't got a crystal fucking ball up under all this, pakeha?' She is dressed extensively in the hand-me-down possum skin clothing of her ancestors with more pouches available to her to hide things than a hobo got pockets. 'They been moving runaways and I wanna know where. I wanna know how. Because you and our little winged friend here have compromised an operation that's been brewing for years.'

'Compromised our fucking operation,' repeats Alice, grinding the butt out in the dirt. Pocketing the stub for later.

'Mukata, settle down,' I say, placating. I know how far she can throw a creature. 'Your power's gonna trigger a djinn storm or, or an earthquake, if yer not—'

'Little Earth, will ya just shut the fuck up for once. Terrence, come with me.'

To everyone else she calls, 'Just go prepare stuff, iwi, eh.'

She forges ahead of the others, up the steps and onto the big rocker on the porch. 'So how do I get a meeting?'

He tells them about the Midnight Express and the-door-that's-not-a-door that opens onto a transport vortex to elsewhere. Explains that they can't get the trailer out of the Slums and that the two of them *are* as much the trailer as the trailer is a person. How? The relationship didn't start out like that but, then, neither of them had known that the silver bullet wasn't simply what she appeared to be. That in the early days that some mad, crazy scientist had merged the DNA of a prehistoric giant of an animal with the chemical compositions of a whole bunch of compounds based on the mathematics of the Einstein-

Rosen Bridge Theory and 3D printed the resulting wormhole to look like a vehicle. That it simply adores Bull and Lil. It had all been in the instruction manual but who reads that until one has a need? The manual was also very clear that the moment the trailer was driven out of the warrens of the old city it would be exposed to elements it was not created to experience. Certain annihilation. Turns out everyone concerned was wrong about that. One sleek chrome T-Rex had a mind of her own, but I get ahead of myself.

'However–' he continues, 'I provide their contact details. And where the hybrid-smugglers take the refugees. The Midnight can only shuffle just so many through her portals before she's whacked anyway.'

'So, Gamble?'

'Mukata?' I ask, a sudden dread washing over me.

'We're ready to go, wahine. Soon as we've established alliances with the city confederacies we do the rescue and make the run.'

I try to look invisible.

'Gamble? Do we have a problem?'

'Ah–'

Here's me. See. All along I've agreed to her crazy idea. Free the hybrids and whoever else they can. Snatch and grab. She and the chiefs've planned it down to the wire, but I don't suppose I was listening. Bar rooms and gin and eternal life require much attention.

That and the occasional trick. Flying on no-moon nights. Awareness of the far-away mountain lakes that still exist at the top of the world.

Predating on small mammals, and male mantises after mating. The sheer pleasure of shedding an outmoded exoskeleton. Ootheca on the branches of tall trees. I sigh. Not for one moment did I think they'd decide to do it.

'Don't you go anywhere, Little Earth. You just stay put,' she threatens, before turning her attention to Alice.

'Whatcha get, sweetheart?'

'Five pigs and a bag full of what we think are chickens. They're gen-mod so who the fuck really knows. Too small for turkeys, though. Plus, Tommy raided the hydro joint.'

He grins, exposing stainless steel teeth. 'Took the veggies and the pots as well.'

'That's me boy. Paint, how many ponies we got up in the high paddocks?'

'Two, maybe two and a half thousand.'

'How many be rideable you think?'

'I'll only risk half, Ma.'

'Fair enough, hoa. And Alice...' Alice stops unloading supplies. 'Alice, how many pirates and gunslingers you can round up from Dodge what's packin?'

'All of em.'

'Grand. I can use that. Gamble? You, me and Terrence in the lab.'

'I'll have my cuppa tea before I go,' Alice insists, leaping the steps ahead of us and wiping his boots on the welcome mat. 'Kettle's boiling its guts out.'

We settle up in front of the stove on hard-back chairs. Mukata produces a jug of her newest batch of tequila with the micro-dose shot of psilocybin she's famous for and Alice, happy now, glides towards the outside with a tin mug of steaming English Breakfast tea.

While the community of Constance falls to action preparing their belongings for what might just be a very long time, Paint dances, summoning up an intelligent djinn storm to cover our tracks.

13

RQ-27 Shadow UAV and the Summit of '26

(Alice)

AFTER THE MOST OF THE OIL RAN out international travel was rooted. Most everybody before that had had internet and cars and… well you probably don't know what I'm talking about but it's all there in the badlands. If you hunt for it. We did and still do. People used to fly inside huge metal cylinders with wings. Stop laughing. There are so many things that we're never told about. People could text on telephones. Men had the ends of their dicks cut off coz they were supposed to be unclean and women had to get their breasts enlarged. Surgeons would cut open the underneath of them, pull up all the tissue and muscle and insert plastic bags full of silicone. I kid you fucken not. Then sew them up again. I could write a book on what I know, I tell ya.

Blokes like me were not supposed to fall in love with other blokes like me and in some parts of the world we were stoned to

93

death for it. And the only reason I'm currently unattached is cause I can't ravish my fucken tank, can I?

What was I saying?

People typed entire conversations with their thumbs onto those heretofore mentioned phones. To all over the world. I've seen the tech. An entire generation ended up hunchbacked because of it. Cause of bending over the fucken things all day. Okay. I'll shut up about this, but the point *is* the war. My god, that fucken war! And you know how Wonderland sends out drones searching for runaways and vagabonds and us pirates and the like? Well, back a hundred years ago or so the military used them to bomb people to death. Oh, got your attention now, have I? Not only bombs, but lasers. I've got me a whole library of data *and* the tech to read it.

Things got everso-moresomely dreadful when the wells went dry. Just like that. Poof! And when the oil ran out nothing moved anymore. What countries' 1%ers saw it coming and took control of what was left. Which is how come the pipelines to and from the Atlantic are off limits, with death being the outcome to all those silly pricks what try the runs. And they still do, mind. Word spreads through the airwaves and ley lines and cockroaches, and other bugs like Gamble, like mainlining. Us wildlife never got noticed for our ability to know this shit so it's only humans in the dark.

Well, the dicks in cities like Wonderland had a summit way back in 2126. They agreed to dismantle weaponized drones. Ballistic and intercontinental missile systems flopped like a lame sideshow at a cheap carnival and the F/A-48 Super Hornets, used to disperse drone swarms over Damascus, what? A kazillion fucken miles away from us and propaganda'd to be the enemy because ya can't justify the cost of that much fire power, at the expense of shelters for the homeless and any kind of health care and women's rights and gay pride without an enemy, can you? And ya can't blast babies to death anymore in ancient places like Syria if ya can't fly a plane.

Point is, we're just about to make the run of a lifetime and I think we can do it. I THINK WE CAN FUCKEN DO IT because even though the drones can track us they can't kill us. It's gotta be their people what kill us. And I think they forgot how to do it in the wild so I'm fucken ECSTATIC!

14

To Ride a Pale Horse

(Gamble)

MUKATA'S GOT A RIDE OF HER OWN. BIG enough for her buxomness, beneath that pile of dead possum. It's a 2087 Indian. Massive power plant displacing 1811cc, kicking out 100bhp and 139Nm torque. She can heft it like it's a small child and loves it like one as well. Her grandmother's ride. Dents and gouges and band aid wiring. She's kept it alive with bootleg grease from Dodge. Driven on an ethanol recipe her koroua left his kids and grandkids before he composted into landscape. It was all he had but Earth, what an inheritance. Paint can go whisper the horses into the conspiracy. Those that agree to come will come. He'll abide by that. The high country just outside of Constance is the only safe place for them. As far as Paint or anyone else knows these are the last, living, anywhere. But before he does that he will cover our backs with his sand dance.

'You got about three hours afore the blow,' Paint says softly from just inside the door of the storeroom where the bikes are housed.

'We're going right now,' says Terrence.

Mukata guns the Indian.

Vroom, Terrence ignites the Guzzi, me on pillion. I'm still woman and this time he does a little jiggle when my breasts make contact with his back. Arms round him, holding tight.

'You sure you can do this without us?' says Paint, worried.

'No.'

'Keep eyes in the back of your head then, Ma.'

Out along the Razorback, keeping to tracks that me and Mukata can see but Terrence is blind to 'cause we gotta ride in the Indian's dust. Under cover of rugged tall cliffs and a day full of strange fog, the old woman's weather magic, ahead of the djinn storm. Drones can't fly in a pea-souper. Can't navigate in any kinda damp.

Corporate big boys never had any luck manipulating the weather. They did try. Been at it for years. Best fuckin trick they could have, if they could've. Tried seeding rain, in the years we still had it. Mukata's been at this fog business like all her ancestors. It's a Long White Cloud thing. They can summon agreement with underground aquifers the government's got no knowledge of. Indigenous folk always know where the water is. Dams were never going to cut it. And because they been consistent forever, no one, not anywhere, questions whether it is anything more than an inexplicable anomaly comes out of nowhere. Same as the desert girls and boys and the djinn storms. Children of the Simpson, of the Sonora, sons of the Sahara. Daughters of the Gobi. We got that magic within us, only we have not forgotten. We have not thought of ourselves as separate somehow from weather and soil. That's too bizarre to contemplate. It makes the wings within my skin ache just thinking about it.

Riding out of the valley I notice the sentries're gone. There'll be nobody to find once the drones are back airborne. So, the only thing we have to do now is liberate the hybrids and humans trapped in a no-man's land of corporate abandonment. Not that many now because most of them died off during the famine of two years ago and the remaining few thousand have pretty much given up.

Well, we'll see. It's up to Terrence to deliver now. At least with Mukata along we can do invisible. She has this light-bending trick her people developed a century ago to fool the cops that there were no dope plants when the front yard was full of them. A kind of Māori feng shui they call *marama piko*.

15

Deliverance

(Terrence)

MUKATA, GAMBLE AND I JUST MAKE IT to the storm water tunnel with moment to spare. A wall of sand and grit howls across the sky from a hundred miles away and turns day to night. Nothing's going to hear our rumble while this keeps up. Headlights strobing the blackness, we cruise the shafts below the old city mile after mile, navigation easy because my memory. And I see maps as patterns, so... two lefts, right, straight, ignore side tunnels for 1.35 kilometers, left, left again and so on till we're under the Strip in the Slums where the Midnight Express is parked this week.

We kill the engines and I take the lead up the ladder to the grate, pushing it aside easily. Gamble's out behind me but then I realize Mukata is having a hard time in the small cylinder, so we sit down to wait, in the gutter. When she finally surfaces she's swearing in Maori and sweating in her possum-skins, but she shakes herself down and within seconds checks out the lay of the land, the look on her face one of horror.

I didn't know it then, because Gamble is slack on details at the best of times, but Mukata has never even been to Dodge, let alone its old city, which is where Alice and the raiders find their info and tech. Where I found mine. Talk about sensory shock. Neon flashing and streetlamps. Even some of the shops still have electricity.

Bull sees us through the window and mouths *Hang on,* before moving out of sight. When he opens the door the air's as thick as clotting blood and the music's pumping. The dance floor is packed and the air stinking from the vapor of countless synth e-pipes is like an assault. He uses himself as a battering ram to get us to the other side of the bar and out through the back door to the annex.

Rattlesnake Lil is playing chess with a hybrid that could be anything canid mixed with person. It's also beating the pants off her and she's not a good loser.

'Later, bitch,' she hisses, lifting the savage pinky ring in threat.

The coyote-person stands, stretches and saunters down the alley in the direction of a dumpster backing onto the Vietnamese café, its tail a flag of contempt, its middle finger in the air in reply.

'This better be pertinent,' she snarls at me, 'I was just about to land my winning move. Who're they and why are they here?'

Then she catches Gamble's scent and staggers, almost falls.

'Are you what I think you are? A piece of forever?'

Gamble doesn't know quite how to respond.

'Um…'

'What am I?' mumbles Mukata, dropping her bulk onto the coyote-hybrid's seat, 'fucken invisible?'

'Bull, Lil, this is Mukata, Mother of the town of Constance out in the Badlands, and this is Gamble, a skellig.'

'A skellig?' says Rattlesnake.

'Long story.' Gamble leans against the doorframe, holding out, 'but literally nobody's ever marked me before so how?'

'I'm a *wuyu*, immortal. Do I bow?'

'You feelin awed you can get me a bottle of gin and a shot glass. Please.'

'Make mine tequila with shroom, thanks anybody,' grins Mukata, taking up the entire bench seat that runs along the chrome wall and packing herself a pipe 'And you got any mice I can eat *before* you barbeque them?'

'What? You prefer them raw?' I guffaw, embarrassingly, in a snorting little way, not knowing, but getting the hint with her stare.

When the hackles have all been soothed and enough alcohol consumed for there even to be a little jollity, Mukata explains everything and asks for their help.

She is assured that she will have it.

16

Nutters' Night – One Week Later

(Gamble)

THE DEAD ZONE IS KNOWN BY AMBULANCE drivers and paramedics, other emergency services and nurses worldwide as being three in the morning. It's always a nuisance but it's when people are woken by unrecognizable screams, murders, mass shooters coked up to the eyeballs or off their faces on pharmas for PTSD because the wars have left their insides riddled with fear and uselessness. Suicides. Car crashes. ODs. King hits by pissed up party boys. Rape in every way conceivable, and more deaths in homes and hospitals than at any other time. It's not peaceful, but it is handy when you want distraction. Within the outlaw community is a network that cooperates, when it needs to, like a termite mound. This was the time temporary truces were revoked, old grievances revived, vengeances taken, enemies topped, gang law imposed and every arsonist out on bail given a cigarette lighter as long as what they burned was in Wonderland and not out here in the Slums.

Mukata, Terrence and Bull lead the liberation. A crew of gunslingers from Dodge, shape-shifters and hybrids from Constance, blood warriors and shamans, and Blackbird, Mukata's liberated little female-looking transdroid whose freedom she bought from a sole trader a couple of years back. It's been reprogrammed from sexual pleasure droid to hacker and Mukata had paid through the nose knowing how big a plus that could be for the plan. It would be needed if they were to have any chance of breaching the lab security.

Me? It was the wrong cycle of the moon for me, sky as black as a corporate head's heart, so I'm stuck with wings, antennae and compound eyes. All I can do is reiterate what I know happened. Terrence and the others had to carry out the freedom raid without me.

So...

Nutters' night began on Bing-Wu, 29, 4864. That's June, 2156 on our old calendar afore it changed to Chinese. The rustlers hustled through the storm water drains until they grouped just under the facility where Terrence and I first met. He couldn't use his barcode.

Disappearing for this many days usually meant either a scientist had gone rogue or was dead. Alarms would light up like disco glitter across every major police and special ops databank. No. It was to be as subtle as butter and that meant Blackbird and her innate technology gained them entry: a ghost whispered along the wires and the monitors went down; a moth landed on the heat pad and an image identifier was knocked out. That did not, unfortunately, include human private security forces, so blood was sure to flow. The guards were aware of intrusion and were packing enough weapons for a war; Kevlar-armored to the max. Sure, they had firepower, but our people also had firepower.

We also had fangs and talons enough, and so corridor after corridor we outnumbered them a hundred to one. Brain and bone and blood splattered those nice antiseptic chrome and white hallways in some strangely Rorscharchian artistic animism. That latter being Alice's description.

Once past the temporary containment arenas they are in. Mile after mile of electric fencing, vast barracks, computer-controlled guard towers… And misery. Housing the down and out, hybrids due for termination, and reservations of people and mutants. All destined for either organ harvesting or soylent green. The down-and-out left to starve and rot, for later use as compost. Our convoys unlocking them, gathering them. Leading them away to safety.

All that time I was stuck in the back of the bar of the Midnight while Lil kept up the business end of things to a room full of the wild, wild west, spellbound by the honeyed tonsils of Sapphire Sepultura, rum-skinned seductress; one of the few surviving burlesque babes wielding ostrich feather fans from a hundred years ago, singing *Do the Watusi*, legendary ballad as gold today as it ever was.

Just when everything seemed hunky dory the Midnight Express gunned her motor of her own accord and lurched from the back annex, an elephant in estrus and hungry for seed. Along Baker Street, almost mowing down the punters. Tables were scattered, glasses and patrons sailed through the air and Sapphire's fabulous naked arse was exposed for all to see, those feathery guardians of modesty downed for the sake of grabbing at something solid.

Just as Lil got up front to where she could take over manual control the vehicle stopped. Through the open intercom, the voice of the GPS says, *At the next corner all passengers will vacate the premises. At the next corner all passengers will vacate the premises.* Then it reared again and charged along the street scattering visitors onto the sidewalks along the way.

Lil grabbed the microphone saying, 'Management apologizes to our guests for the inconvenience. There has been an emergency and we must ask you to all bugger-off as quick as you can when we stop. We hope to be back on Sunset Strip within twenty-four hours. Thank you.'

The Midnight parks herself at the corner and let everyone out. I was hiding. Didn't know what to do. Rattlesnake came to my cubby and whispered to sit tight. She'd work out what the fuck was going on soon enough.

Bull needs me, said Midnight through the GPS, slamming her doors and revving her motor.

'What the fuck?' cussed Rattlesnake.

Rattle, sit up front with me and I'll explain everything. And Gamble? My little runway? This one's for you. The jukebox lifted a vinyl and dropped it onto the stack. You gotta wonder where she found all these classics. I was impressed. The girl band the Crystals from way back before the famine years sang *He's a rebel and he'll never ever be any good, he's a rebel cause he never ever does what he should…* And I was transported to a golden age. I remembered Harley Davidsons, silk and ink wells. Hell, I remembered Mozart.

It was Midnight doing the talking. It all came out. Her being a hybrid and keeping a low profile or else. That now the run for the border was on, she was going to be necessary.

17

Years Ago – The Plan

(Gamble)

IN THE OLD CITY. In the forgotten, moldy libraries and what could be gleaned from purloined technology still readable. That had been Alice and Rottie's work for decades. But not just theirs. Bull'd been told the story by Early Lewis, who'd heard it from his mammy, who'd heard it from hers and so forth. Said it was a cold land though what *cold* was no one knew. Said it was a white land, a mountain and forest land, not dust and sand and wind-grass like the badlands. Rivers and lakes, not the tapped underground aquifers or the rehydrated water under the domes. Other. Snow. Ocean that was alive. Volcanoes that blew their tops and spewed fire from the core of mother earth, and had always done, creating arching vaults called lava tubes. Animals were protected, and bears were real bears. Chickens had legs and laid eggs. Other species of no use to people at all just hung out in peace. Dug burrows, built nests. Lived in the soil. Land of the Midnight Sun is what it's known as because some of the year is never dark.

I'd educated Mukata and the others, bout what I know, long time ago. Mukata said it sounded like where she grew up. Ngāi Tahu, on the island of Aotearoa, across the sea so far south it was like the north. I told her of a river between this land and that. Big deep, raging, mother of a river. No labs. No factory farms. Alice questioned how come the military haven't got their mitts on it forever ago. I explained the border was—maybe is—guarded by an ancient race called the Álfur, and there's no getting past them they don't agree to the transaction. That they're the Grace's lot.

I lived amongst them when they realized. A thousand years ago. They saw into the future and were horrified. They closed the border. Reversed what damage had been done. Taught the people to rewild the fuck outa that landscape. And it's big. Vast. Then the Álfur set to an endless vigil beside that river.

Everyone asked me what the Álfur are and I couldn't explain other than to say they're like me, but they never change. That they are everything that makes up the landscape and everything that lives within it and they were already there when the first two-legged people slimed themselves out of the mud and learned to walk. You might call them the spirits of place. Or ghosts. Or ancestors. Maybe people, maybe intelligent fog. Except they hit hard. With weather hoodoo. Can freeze a person in seconds.

'What's freeze?' Ragtime had asked.

'Glaciate,' I'd replied.

'You what?'

'Fucken dead, is what.' I'm such a know-it-all sometimes. Not outa meanness, just fun is all.

'So,' said Mukata.

'So,' I replied, settling down with a fresh cuppa coffee.

'We'd have to run the river, we wanna get those critters free.'

'You think the ghosts will let us come?' First time I seen fear in Paint's eyes.

18

Ahu Paruru Mata

(Mukata)

THE *AHU PARURU MATA*, IS a little like a blindfold. But it's a deformity in the brain.

There's more than one species of people. The ones with ahu paruru mata do all the hurting because they think they are separate from life. Cut down the first forests because they can. Call trees lumber. Use decimation and call it necessary war. Keep on cutting the life out of earth without hearing the screaming. Pen four-legged people in places where they can't move. They don't understand the terror. That they know what's going on. Once their grandmothers roamed grasslands and grazed and every now and then someone would spear a male. Cut his throat till he was dead if the spear didn't do the job. Skin him, carve him up, share him out amongst the other people, tan his hide and sew it into clothing or tents or moccasins then carve his bones for the needles to sew with. Use him for hoes and awls. For flutes and jewelers and scoopers and hide-grainers. I could go on but you get my meaning. People took down a bull or a ram or a kangaroo with balls because a cow could be pregnant and that was taboo.

They ate grass, not corn.

Fish didn't have no mercury.

No antibiotics or hormones in chickens.

Chickens used to eat bugs outside in the garden and gardens were tended by gardeners. We had wild fruit. The world had elephants, and if you don't know what them is, nor orangutans neither, then all the sadder for you. And each and every everything that felt. They still do.

Those poor little monkeys with the electrodes on their exposed brains, those poor rabbits with air purifier in their eyes. Those poor everythings being harvested for their parts with no anesthetic because it's too expensive to justify. The vast fields of corn and grain and soy beans and sugar cane for either biofuel or food substitute, stifling everything that used to live wild and unpoisoned.

And those of us *without* the ahu paruru mata know that. We communicate with each other. Always have. *Brer Rabbit* and *Winnie the Pooh* taught the white kids about cunning and justice and friendship. *Mowgli* knew it. Jeremy, in that old movie *Powder*, knew it.

Shape-shifters in every village. The skins of eagles, the hides of elk foretelling when to plant, what would heal. Walkers tracking every landscape mapped out by ancestors, in standing stone, the shape of headlands, the chatter or calamity of mother river or brother boulder. Our uncles who are mountain chains and bottomless lakes, cousins who are prevailing winds and ocean currents, children who are the first frost, ash spewing from grandmother volcano warning us where not to camp too long. Ants before a quake, spiders before a flood. One big gathering, is earth. One long song. One important conversation.

But the two-legged people with ahu paruru mata hear only themselves. Get lost. Rely. Pretend to be better than other people of any species from ferned to feathered. Somebody really fucked up when they brainwashed the first of them. Then, if you don't know how to take off the blindfold? Well, that's this world of suffering, and this is why we hope what Gamble told us of the lands north of the river, north of the border, are true, eh? There isn't any going back, and we better get used to the cold up there because she's going to freeze again and if we're here in the badlands or trapped in those corrals when she comes we won't be ready. Not this time. I remember all this through my ancestors' stories. Little Earth remembers because she was there. That's why I put up with her, otherwise, who would?

Metua vahine, warn your children, eh?

19

The Whole Shebang

(Gamble)

Midnight kept her vigil, letting Bull and Rattlesnake Lil run the show. But now was the big beast's moment. Now's when she could let rip.

And she did. She was out of the Slums and barreling down the old freeway away from the dome at a hundred and ten, headlights cutting across ancient abandoned wreckage and maneuvering like she was doing the shimmy.

We finally pull over at the top of the hill behind the fractured, borer-riddled *HLWD* sign and the Midnight Express quiets to an idle, growling, the low rumble of a tiger, waiting. She's limited. She's always known that. She can only send the escaped through the portal one at a time but if the rest could survive the run to Constance they stood a chance.

Here they come, whispers the Midnight, at the roar of two motorcycles and the thunder of a thousand pair of feet or hooves or whatever. Rattlesnake and me are out the door fast as yesterday. Her with diagonal pliers to cut a big enough hole in that god-awful fence to make a difference and me, taking to the air, scenting for Terrence amidst the milieu.

(Terrence)

UP AHEAD I SEE THE MIDNIGHT EXPRESS and Lil slicing open that awful fence. Overhead I hear Gamble peep-peeping in that eagle voice of hers and know she's got my back. The Midnight Express then bends all the light the rest of us could never see and she seems to vanish. Waiting, willing and ready, to disappear the refugees that might be left when the law gets wind.

With the strength of ten, Rattlesnake Lil bends back the chain link fence. A maw of liberation where a wall of hate had stood for a millennium. And we're through, straight past Lil, out onto the badlands.

That shrill, impossible whistle I associate with Paint splits the night and a battalion of fifty heavily armed squaws ride ahead of the pack and dismount at a run, heading to Midnight, weapon-ready, their ponies keeping pace.

Rattlesnake Lil joins them, ushering hybrids, people and mutants into Midnight, still not knowing whether they'd live or die just that they *would* do it free.

Mukata, Bull and I ride hard. Behind us a wall of dust almost as high as a djinn storm, but isn't, bleeds the starlight from the night. They haven't yet seen the Airstream.

I turn to Mukata and I know my eyes are like a rabbit's under hunter floodlights.

'All the pretty horses, pakeha,' she yells, white teeth grinning for the first time since I met her.

If I squint I can just recognize Paint and Ragtime. They're up front of a bareback crew of many-hued people who've lived with these lands in a symbiotic relationship, oh, probably since the world began. And they're followed by a herd of what must be easily a thousand horses.

Taking up both flanks is the convoy of trucks and rhinos a'bristle with weaponry. Alice has the hatch of the rhino open, proudly and boldly wearing a yellow floral frock.

Behind us, way back in the distant memory that is Wonderland, sirens wail.

(Gamble)

'We're fucked,' Terrence wails in my direction, his voice cracking. Poor Good Hair man.

Then whoah, the moon flips to new even though it'll be three days till that first sliver of fingernail will be seen, and it's transformation time. And it's just like Dodge. Wings and tits. I swoop from the sky onto the pillion of the Guzzi scaring the shit outa my boyfriend because he hasn't seen me fully change my skin before.

'Shut up Terrence,' I murmur, nuzzling his neck as the morph completes itself. 'Let's discuss it if things get tore up.'

Humans are a funny species like that. They don't understand a thing they get angry. Some even get angry enough they kill the thing they're scared of. Well, historically, that'd be sub-continents, wouldn't it? Take sharks. They were around, perfect, for a few million years. Then I remember when they killed off the last one. I wept that day. I try to never cry, trust me. That's a thing about being all woman that just doesn't back down. Once a month nothing's funny.

20

Mō tātou, ā, mō kā uri, ā muri ake nei
For us and our children after us

(Alice)

'MUKATA?' I yell from the yard. Park the rhino and jump down into the fucken dust that's teeming with runaways and horses, warriors setting up fires in the center of town, and healers from out in the badlands and up in the high country makin their way from one damaged individual to the next. Doesn't serve a person to wear a decent frock to a rescue, now does it? Look at me? My fucken nails are filthy, and I've got a six o'clock shadow. 'Mukata? You in there?' I call towards the lab. No answer so I head for the shed where she keeps the Indian. Knowing her she'll be up to her elbows in grease after last night.

'Knock, knock, Ma. You in there?'

Terrence pulls the doors open and goes to throw his arms around me and I stop him just in time. Yes, they're workin on the bikes, no I'm not in the fucken mood till I've changed.

'Crowd's building and I think you're gonna have to do something before we run outa food. You want me and the battalion to head out raiding?'

'Ow.' Old tohunga stands and stretches her back, a bandana keepin her hair from her eyes and the rare sight of the chief in raggedy old coveralls, sleeves rolled up to the elbows, snake and lizard ink twining both leathery arms. 'Fuck, Alice, you're a mess.'

I pull the last of the best cigar I've smoked in a decade from my bum bag and light it, waiting for the green light, ignoring the insult.

'Look, don't stress and go get changed. Have a shave, for fuck's sake, Alice. By then I'll've got the chain back on and I'll be able to better interpret the situation.

I hear the rumble of the Airstream off in the distance and realize there'll be an even bigger crowd by now.

'Terrence, where's Gamble?'

'In the lab with Paint.'

'Doing what?'

'No idea.'

'Good, she can be on cuppas. I need a fucken bath.'

(Mukata)

Bull comes out of the Midnight Express just as I finish up washing my hands. He's followed by hybrids and people, one after the other, stumbling and helping each other, following Lil to the medical station down the street at what used to be the old pub.

'Kia ora,' I welcome, 'thank fuck you made it. Hey Midnight,' and I wave to the bus.

Bull then puts his massive hands on my shoulders and leans down for the gentlest hongi ever, eh? I understand what the little China woman sees in a cowboy like this. He just knows. Then I step back to gauge the crowd because there's some crazy hybrid mixes here. What them scientists trying to make anyway? People coyotes, people gorillas, remember gorillas? Peopledroids, people with blue skin, skin like a crocodile, no noses, just holes like snakes. Whole bunch with parietal eyes and gills in their necks. Sort of reminds me when they used to cut the tails off Dobermans and slice the ears off pit bulls. Supposed to be practical. Doesn't matter how cruel. Lot of these people been bred for underwater work too dangerous for ordinary divers. Or the arenas, I think, cause of the scars. Otherwise what else could have marked them that bad? Your stock standard human people seem the worse off. Not saying a word. No facial expressions. That so they don't get picked? I think of the work ahead of us if we get them to sanctuary. If.

'What happened? How come they didn't go through?' says Terrence, indicating the stragglers.

'Midnight's wasted. Temporarily anyway. We're all of us same, about now. Least she can shelter a hundred or more for the run to the river. Protection when the ackack starts up.'

'Java's on,' says Gamble from the door of the lab in our direction. 'Alice's orders.'

When Lil returns the three of us go into the lab and I fill em in on some gaps.

Paint and Ragtime chop and sort the Little Mothers, from peyote to fly agaric, for the people and their customs. For tonight. It's time to dance themselves into their true shapes to call the starman, John Inapertwa, from wherever he is. To entice him here to help us. He's another piece of the Grace that broke away, like Gamble, from the red rock of Kata Tjuta. A thousand years ago. He was curious to track the dragon lines of the world. I know for a fact the strange lightning the day the ground rumbled was him waking up from being some rock somewhere or some piece of sky.

He's our wayshower. Gonna take us home.

21

There's a Starman…

(Gamble)

IT'S LONG AFTER THE CEREMONIES AND dances. I'm as pissed as a loon on moonshine and off my face from the psilocybin in the last shot, loving up the fire. I musta sat for what would have been hours, sharing stories of the long ago, with my fellow virtuous and unjustly imprisoned vagabonds of variable and uncertain origins. Of the Tuatha Dé Dannan and Cúchullain, the Fíana and those fucking monks that made my mind up for me to shift into a new shape. Love a captive audience that couldn't give a shit what I look like. That don't possess prejudice. Mukata hoodooed up a mist way earlier, just after sunset, so I'm in a whole lot of bliss, my wings little bits of rainbow, laying down my back just like when I got nabbed and met Terrence. Not quite all woman but close. Morning will see me fully skin.

It's quiet now, so I'm communing with the hums and chirrups of night, the feel of a low sky, the smell the earth gets when it's been radically dry and now it's not. Life sneaking a concept of *perhaps*, from seeds like stars, buried just inches below my bum, buried for all those savanna years because people screwed up so righteously back then.

Blackbird's off to the edge of town practicing riding that little fifteen hand high Galloway pony that Paint gave her. He even gifted her a real leather saddle cause she ain't built to sit a horse. She's getting good. She'll have to be to keep up. Most determined little droid I ever did see. Mukata like a mother she never had.

Terrence is gone with Alice and the convoy way along the valleys and buttes towards Wonderland. For when, not if, the military deploys. Cause, fuck me, the empire must be mad as a nest of hornets hit with a stick by now. Mukata, Paint, Ragtime, Rotti, Rattlesnake, Bull and a couple of hundred other warriors are sentried all along the cliff tops. Knowing the drones'll be scouring the badlands in swarms. Not here yet, the mist fucking with their mechanisms and radars and such. Maybe they're even out there to give the starman a rouse of a welcome when he decides to arrive. But that's not what happens.

It's like a piece of mist breaks away, clinging to the backs of the two. One is the music man from the Midnight Express, head down, black Stetson hiding his eyes for now, guitar case in a be ringed hand. The other, dressed in jeans, long black curly hair covered mostly by a thick dirty-grey hoodie, his fists buried deep in the pockets, his face daubed in white and ochre clay, eyes of anger and starlight but the colors of bark and the dark North Sea. Barefoot. He looks down at me as they arrive at the fire pit.

'John Inapertwa is him,' says the music man. 'The starman. And he don't bother with talk so I'm the bard what does so on his behalf. Name's Justice by the way. You Gamble?'

'I'm Gamble,' I say standing, my wings stridulating automatically out of excitement. Legends are what I live for. Untold stories. And I don't know these two creatures that happen to look almost like men. I only know what Mukata has said of the wayshower, and who knows if that's truth or someone's explanation of the way magic works?

'You a chunk of rock too, I hear,' I smile.

He laughs. If I wasn't so fucking in love with Terrence I could be turned on by that alone, a precious sound redolent of when there was an autumn.

'I can talk to you, Little Earth,' he says softly, surprising Justice who pushes his hat back and lifts his brows, displaying the palest blue eyes I ever seen.

'Yeah I'm a bit of rock. Old as volcanoes, just like you.' He sits beside me. I notice that none of the sleepers lying about Constance stir at all. A spell laid over everyone.

'You do this?' I ask, gesturing to the bodies everywhere.

'You and Mukata keep the whole lot of them away from us when they wake. We need alone, you understand. They're sure to make enough noise to break the air, I know they will. And then the guns will start the killing.'

'We won't get clean away?'

He doesn't answer.

'Will we make it across the river? Can you at least tell me that?'

'Might as well ask life to be fair. The Grace is just the Grace and I'm not a seer. Not my job. Ain't no such thing as fate just like there ain't no thing as right.' He pauses, and I can hear the trucks in the distance as well.

'But there is wrong.' He bends and scoops a handful of ash from the perimeter of the fire pit. Rubs it into his hair under the hoodie, adds it to his face. Holds my hand for a moment, leaving it grey with meaning. Some critters, like these two, seen too much of the hurt. I get it.

'How's your sense of smell? Your hearing?'

'As good as yours,' I say.

'We need to be at least a day ahead of you, way ahead,' says Justice, 'so keep your nose on our scent and your ears open for my strings. You, understand?'

'Where you from, Justice?' I ask. The unrecognizable something in his expression being not... not worldly somehow. Like a piece of myth.

'I'm from where you're going. I'm the ice what's still left to cool the Grace. I'm from a million years ahead and I know what the world is like when those seasons have ringed more trees than there is sand on the ocean floor.'

'Is it terrible?'

'It's beautiful. And the stars look very different.'

John Inapertwa stands, and the two men walk back into the mist as though they've never been. But I've got the smell in my nostrils. And pickle this, I'm weeping because I'd forgot, it's been so deep into the long ago and not what I expected. Just goes to show people shouldn't second guess. I thought he'd smell of desert because of his origins.

But I got spruce. And I got rowan. And I got mountain oak and holly and elms and apples and beech forests. Tundra. The scent of raging water coming six hundred feet off the edge of a mountain, that metallic thing that happens around wet rock. That briny perfume that comes from kelp trapped shoreside of a coastal shoal, not a hint of plastic in any of it. Grace, I can smell seals and I can smell the musk of elk and the damp fur on the backs of hunting wolves. Salmon cooking over an open fire. Starman? Fuck me, I'm homesick. So yes, I can follow this forever if needs be. And Justice? If you can play the classics from the old days when we had hope? Again, forever. Because I'd forgotten about that thing. We all had.

22

Your sons and your daughters are beyond your command

(Gamble still talking)

PICKLE THIS AND FUCK THAT IS ALL I am thinking as the rhinos move in while it's still dark, waking the dreamers, the spell lifted, the visions that enticed the starman drifting like yesterday. We're this close and all I can do is fear. Not for me. How can I fear for me? I'm eternal. Immortal. No. For this lot that's breaking my heart. Because of the river to freedom a day or two away at least and a militia intent on the destruction of every life here; an end to the embarrassment.

The starman's smells swirl like gossamers through me. He said there is wrong and yes, he is fair to say so. But for every wrong there is a witness that knows what really happens. A storyteller who keeps shtum when the politics and the propaganda of the day determine to

133

suffocate, gas, starve, humiliate, belittle, diminish or outright strike true events from historic accounts. While the starman is a wayshower, Justice is a bard and, fuck it, for the sake of you left to read this, so am I. Two jobs. That's all I got in the entirety of my foreverness so far: follow my nose and tell the truth about all this. The first selfless things I've ever done. Because so much of this wrong has yet to get fixed.

At the hour before dawn we've got twelve hundred humans and thirty-five hundred hybrids and mutants ready to take to such an unknown land. Cause I ask myself: if I'm off my face did I imagine those two men? Is the smell conjured out of hope? Does it matter? No. And fifteen hundred horses. Warriors gather around Paint, hooting and hollering just like John said they would, stirring up the dust now the fog has dried with the daylight. Every cowboy from Dodge, even the saloon owners and their kin, all here for the fun of riding for real and a chance to shoot at something other than rabbits, rats and a cue of sixteen colored balls. Blackbird dressed like a bloke and proud as a droid can be, on her little pony, eyes wide, looking for and not finding Mukata in the swell of everything.

Alice takes the lead. He's kilted up in heavy duty cammos, his chest and shoulders draped with bullet belts, diamond studs in each defiant ear, puffing his stogie to the wind like a war pipe. He's followed by a hundred and five trucks and recycled armored vehicles from a century ago, all powered on Mukata's grandfather's biofuel recipe, and his rainbow flag is a pennant atop a fifteen-foot long standard, blowing proud in the gusty day. Bull and Rattlesnake Lil and the Midnight Express are packing hundreds into the bar, those too beaten or weird to know what to do with legs. The ones that would frighten the horses or those frightened of them. Then Bull joins them mounted on something maybe eighteen hands high, prancing, just like in the olden days.

Mukata's got Ragtime riding pillion, and this time, cause my nose is so damn special, I get to gun the Guzzi, Terrence at my back packing every weapon he can use.

We head out into the badlands followed a few miles back by all the firepower the empire's police and militia can savage, their thousand or more drones flying in the advance.

Stand a chance?

Sometimes and for sometimes in history, you got to take them once or twice. Live or die, it's the same to the Grace. It's the how that seems to me to be the importance.

This is like nothing I've ever experienced. A mile-high wall of red and grey dust. And not a djinn storm, just the ground responding to this much traffic. Behind me gunfire. Mortar fire. Are there people dying back there? I can't. Can't think about that. Got to follow the smells. To trust that these people can maybe also fight. Been what? A hundred or more years since any real war? Those hot doggeties only ever used their weapons on the weak, and they're shooting at us from miles back, silly fucks. They don't know what they're doing is what I think. This little throb of joy bubbles in me. What is that? Compassion? Oh, Gamble, get a grip. First, you're in love with a mortal now you care for these people? You're a lump of rock in drag! But no, it's not something I even want to suppress.

Night. No fires allowed. Me and Terrence down a few shots of moonshine and head out amongst the rocks to fuck our brains out. Something about adrenaline, I suppose. In all my time as a faux person, neither man or woman or mix of anything else got me off like the good haired science boy with the basket-ball hoop on his mother's stage. I asked him once if he studied it or something, but he just dove down between my legs and his answer was muffled so I never found out. Having someone laugh inside you is the very best of buzzes, though, and he's still coming up with surprises. Dear sun and moon, may I never turn when we're doing this, I'd hate to bite his head off.

Day three. I thought we'd have arrived already. We'll be running outa ethylene, despite the reserves in the trucks, we keep going nowhere like this. The enemy is gaining ground and the drone swarms are above all day long like virtual eyes; like virtual wasps. No point shooting at them.

The one thing we all notice is the air. It's cold. And I haven't been this far north on this continent for hundreds of years so even I'm feeling it. Hung about the badlands and Dodge for so many of them I'm even surprised by it. The final morning and I can smell the river for real.

We wake up to frost on the ground. I'm excited but people are scared. Never known it.

'Mukata, wake up,' and she snorts a final snore and rolls outa her swag. I'm sucking on a wad of jerky, in a mood to kill for a cup a java like what Terrence and her can both make. 'People are freaking out. Can you round em all up? Let me talk.'

She and Ragtime take off on the Indian shouting out for a gathering up where Terrence and I wait. When they all come around my first thought is for Alice, body half in, half out the rhino. First time anyone seen him in a shirt.

'Alice? What's the situation with the enemy?'

'They're fuckin gaining on us is the situation. Reckon? They'll hit our rear come nightfall we don't make the crossing. Where the fuck is it and what the hell is this air all about, Gamble?'

I clamber aboard the rhino so I'm high enough for the crowd.

'This is what serious cold is. That's what you're feeling.'

Lot of mumbles like I'm talking gibberish. 'The north feels like this all the time. Freedom's gonna feel like this. You better shut up with the moaning and get to feeling curious cause things are about to get way more intense.'

Terrence and Mukata clamber up beside me.

'Where I came from, once upon a time,' starts Mukata, 'we had this all year. It was clean. We had a relative called hukarere and that means snow.' A sea of confused faces. 'Right. Here's your education and it's short and snappy. Anybody here know the color green?' A few hands go up.

'Well you're all in for surprises, eh? Anybody had the lung disease or seen the sputum from it? Seen a wound go bad?' Lots of hands go up and I stifle a laugh because of how insurmountably ridiculous the world has become. 'In the world of my girlhood green was breathtaking, not sickly. We get further along and the sky's going be the color green. Then it's gonna a drop fucktons a white, soft, coldness onto the landscape and that's also going to be beautiful. Because weather is weather and should be alive and this is where you learn to be you. If we get across the river. If the troopers behind us don't slaughter us. If the guardians on the other side of the border don't reject us and deny us. Give us that will you?' Alice hands her the flask of hooch he's been swilling, and she drains it.

'Better off dead than back there. Anybody wants to turn around now's your chance.'

She hands Alice back the flask. 'You?'

'You kiddin me, Ma? Gamble informed me they don't kill poofters in the north.'

She laughs as she hugs him and spares a possum cape for his shoulders. He shoves the stogie between his teeth, lights it and scarpers back into the rhino with Rotti, ready to rumble.

'Anybody?' yells Mukata.

'Nope,' from the back of the crowd somewhere. And those with horses mount up, including Blackbird who's got it figured out like a native.

We drop to the ground and straddle the motorbikes, pushing the ignition and riding into an overcast day, the metal tang of ice water over stone filling me, along with the faint hint of a slide guitar playing *We are the Champions* from what seems to be a vast distance and a great height.

And finally. Late afternoon under a rainy sky. There it is. A river. A for real, I-kid-you-not, river. Even Terrence is stunned. We pull up a hundred yards away to reconcile what we do next. The drones are gone. Never made to work in the wet. But the sound of militarized vehicles comes closer and closer.

Now the fear is as strong as the hope.

Terrence dismounts and kisses me till, despite the cold and the sheer fucking terror of the situation I'm wet through with lust.

'I'm joining Bull and Paint,' is all he says.

'You ride with me,' I demand.

'Bikes are useless, Gamble.'

It takes me a second to realize I'm an idiot.

'The Midnight?'

'She can swim it. Either get in there with the Rattler or you and Mukata find yourselves a cowboy. You're going to have to double *and* you're going to have to swim.

Now that's a thing I never thought I'd hear. From the raging sea endlessly battering me until I made the change. Never wanted to dip in even a toe. And what hand does the Grace deal me? Told me there'd be a price to pay one day. Well, for dear life, the universe and everything, today's not that day. I find the nearest cowboy and swing up behind him, grabbing hold of his belt, slapping him on the side of the head when he leers like he does at my tits up against his spine.

The Midnight's up front housing the helpless, ready to dive. Many of the mutants and hybrids are braced for the cold once they hit the water. I can sense the resolution. Nothing, before now, matters. The people on horseback are scared. It's palpable. It's as thick as a CEO in the Slums on a Saturday night thinks he'll still have his credits come morning.

As we ride towards the river's edge we see them. Álfur. Thousands of them. Sort of transparent like cellophane, or pale like ghosts or snow. Or ice people. All astride seventeen, eighteen hand pale horses. All carrying weapons like something out of a movie in the ancient of days. Are we dead before we get there?

'Hello!' calls Mukata. No answer.

Where's the starman? Where's Justice when we need him?

Then behind us come the first shots. Close enough. We can't stay here. We're trapped in inevitability. You know the one. That's the time when you can't do nothing. So we ride.

The Midnight Express hits the water like she's a fucking bear or something. Powers out into the deep, raging dark slate water, her hybridization, her dynamic.

The people at the back of the throng are dropping from terrified horses because the slaughter has begun. We ride. Thousands of runaways, hundreds of braves and warriors, hybrids, mutants, the rejected of humanity and those poor little transdroids. The shock of the ice water kills some instantly and they're pulled downstream, rag toys bobbing to an eventual ocean. Horses scream as they are shot. Others gagging at the wetness and just because. But they swim towards the further shore.

Where's Terrence? I can't see him.

Bullets whizz past my head and hit the cowboy, blowing his face off. Nothing to be done and I kick him out of the stirrups, the blood reddening the foam around us before he, too, is dragged downstream.

Where's Mukata? Oh, there she is. Riding with Paint, on his

mountain of a shire horse that can accommodate them both with ease and fording this river like he's done it a thousand times.

Head down, ya fucking skellig. I might be theoretically immortal, but I can be butt ugly with bits of me blown off.

I can just make em out in the mist. The government's men.

Fuck me but they got more fire power than I thought. M988 high explosive mortars. Boom, one of the trucks goes up. Boom another, housing maybe ten people. Humans on the ground now, running. Others like some weird puppets as they dance in the air before dropping dead to the dirt.

I no longer look back. The horse beneath me does not want to die today. She is wheezing with the strain of a will to live. Foam at her mouth, her eyes white around the edges. I lie along her and hum in her ear like we're cantering through a meadow in soft sunshine. I feel her love me.

Where's Bull? I can't see Bull anymore.

Up ahead the Midnight Express makes landfall along with all the mounted squaws. You can see the hesitation. For a split second. Then the Álfur part and twenty turn their horses around gesturing Midnight to follow. They're here to make sure we get across! They're *waiting* for us. The Álfur open fire over our heads, aiming deadly against our persecutors. I make land and we keep on going. There are still hundreds on horseback. Making it to safety. Bullets whizzing. The mortar men are the first the Álfur take down.

Just keep riding.

Just keep going.

'Whishta,' I whisper to the horse in the old tongue, 'whishta, whishta, good gal, whishta now.' And her ears prick forward as the ancientness of her species remembers and knows this is going to work out. Then we're past the firing line. I'm riding with fifty or so others and it's seriously fucking freezing. We're flanked by half a dozen Álfur, stately and ice white, dressed in the finely tooled skin of other pale creatures, tattooed in whorls and dots as blue as a summer sky. Through a forest as green and majestic as Eire before the British raped her for their ships. Then. Ahead. Fire as tall as the fabled giraffe and as wide around as ten of us. Warmth.

Mukata comes running. She holds me and I'm nose-deep in possum fur. 'Little Earth,' she whispers, 'it's all true.'

Rattlesnake Lil opens the door of Midnight and people are met by the androgynous Álfur with warm clothing, gentle smiles.

Alice fords the river in the rhino. Piece of piss. Right up onto the bank. To the flirty smile of the nearest Álfur.

I search the crowd. Paint. Rotti holding Ragtime, her swords loose in both hands. She does a reverse chiburi with one, relinquishing the blood of some stranger into the earth before sliding it into its saya with the experience of a sensei. She doesn't let go of the other.

Justice, over by the longhouse, smoking something thin and black.

That's it. Vomit rising in my throat. I rage into Mukata's face, '*Where's Terrence?*'

We hunt till the last of the stragglers are brought to the throng.

We backtrack to the river. Dead litter the foreshore like autumn leaves. Blood on the stones. Hybrids that thought they could but couldn't. Hundreds mown down.

Where's Terrence?

Across the water the military have reversed. Returning south.

Yeah, go on! Fuck off! You lost. Tails between their legs like the animals they've so harmed. I can only imagine their fate when they get back to the bosses without the mother lode.

Then Bull. He's like a massive mountain of night that's fording the river now the tide is lower. What's he carrying? Is that a sack? I squat and just wait. He wades onto the rocks and stumbles under the weight of his burden.

'I'm sorry,' he says.

Then I understand. The bundle is a man covered in bullet wounds. I don't recognize him. There's fresh blood still running from every gaping hole. Then I see the hand. The tattoo of the bluebird, black blood dripping from the index finger.

I stare at the mess and try to keep breathing but the burn in my chest is a conflagration.

'Someone knew him. Called his name. I think. Doctor Brothers? Someone called. A man in a suit. Terrence Brothers? Was his last name Brothers?'

Bull lowers the body onto my lap and sits. Done in. Two of the Álfur come from the tree-line bringing blankets. Kindness. They drape us both and sit with us.

'He just stands there like he knows,' Bull continues. 'Raises his arms like that crucified guy in the legends. Mukata's little transdroid's pony is shot out from under her. First off, she takes cover behind one of the busted-up trucks but then she runs out into the fire, to try to protect him like she's programmed. Takes the first bullet. It shatters her like she's made of glass.'

'And Terrence?'

'The suit shoots him. Square in the chest. Terrence just stands there as the rest of the people finish the crossing. Like he can take the hits. I'm hiding behind a downed horse that's grunting. Suffering. Dying slow. But what could I do? Somebody has to witness this.

Traitor, screams a suit from his hiding place behind a plas-shield. Behind the armored men. *Fuck you*, yells Terrence as loud as he is able.

The suit and the soldiers opened fire all at once then. Shoot him to smithereens. Once he's down it's like a signal. They'd done what they came to do, and he was the end of it. He was their main target. Then they reversed their vehicles, got em back on the south track and left. Just like that. Job done.

I waited till they was well out of range before shooting the horse. When I got to Terrence he was still alive.

'*Tell Gamble she's the best of them*, he whispered to me, grinning like dying was to be expected. *They wouldn't have come, but I embarrassed them.* That was all he could get out, love. I don't think he was in any pain by then, though. Too close to becoming earth. He got me to bring him to you. Said he needs you to kiss him into tomorrow.'

It begins to snow. White silence. Not hard. Just enough to bless us in the new place. To cover the violence with a softness born of myth. To cover the senselessness of cruelty. Here's the stone of me after all. In me. In the pit of me. The cold of it. The forfeit. White hot coals inside my chest. Destroying me. The depth of it. Then I weep. All this water running down my face to join the song of the river. I have to sit on this rock; have to not move. I can't move. His body is cold. I know it's not Terrence. Terrence is warm. Terrence's eyes are not this dull, dead fish grey. Terrence's eyes are quick-darting. Steamingly erotic. And I just cry. Like a saved person let herself live but lost her soul in the doing. Like a mother must when her children are murdered. The way people must when all the compassion runs out.

One of the Álfur takes Terrence in its arms. As though he weighs no more than a feather. But Bull says no. Help her. Give him to me. He's like a son.

The other Álfur gets me to my feet, embraces me. Loving. He's warm and smells of spruce. I'm surprised by that.

When I'm let go the two of them lead the way home.

THE END

ABOUT THE AUTHOR

Ly de Angeles has been in print since 1987 and is an award-winning author and filmmaker, director and producer of stage and screen, mother, grandmother, scholar, deep ecologist, mythographer, feminist and psychic.

Photograph Anthony Rodriguez, Melbourne, 2017

ABOUT THE COLLABORATOR / ARTIST / EDITOR

Melaine Knight is a musician, performance artist, stylist, costume designer. International Rock 'n Roll Undie Washer, Soothsayer, Velvet Lover guitar slinger and howler. Writer of songs. Creative Director of REBEL REBEL, House of Stylists. Music/film fashion columnist for Red Door Magazine NYC/Copenhagen.

The Neon Rebel

Photographer Theresa Sarjeant